I0690265

Choosing Charity

by

Sara Zavacki-Moore

This is a work of fiction. Names, characters, places, and incidents are either the product of the author's imagination or are used fictitiously, and any resemblance to actual persons living or dead, business establishments, events, or locales, is entirely coincidental.

Choosing Charity

COPYRIGHT © 2022 by Sara Zavacki-Moore

All rights reserved. No part of this book may be used or reproduced in any manner whatsoever without written permission of the author or The Wild Rose Press, Inc. except in the case of brief quotations embodied in critical articles or reviews.
Contact Information: info@thewildrosepress.com

Cover Art by *Debbie Taylor*

The Wild Rose Press, Inc.
PO Box 708
Adams Basin, NY 14410-0708
Visit us at www.thewildrosepress.com

Publishing History
First Edition, 2022
Trade Paperback ISBN 978-1-5092-3803-3
Digital ISBN 978-1-5092-3804-0

Published in the United States of America

"Let's go back to something you said a few minutes ago," Sheila urged. "Remember when you said something to the effect of how you felt heavy? Can you tell me more about heavy?" Anna sighed, leaning back further in her chair. She glanced at the clock, noting the few minutes left in her therapy session.

"Well, it's kinda like when you were a kid at the dentist, and you wore a big lead apron to get an X-ray done. Ya know? I feel like I'm wearing that apron around all the time."

Sheila leaned forward. "Is there anything that makes the apron lighter?"

Anna paused and whispered, "Charity."

Praise for Sara Zavacki-Moore

"*CHOOSING CHARITY* is an insightful and poignant story about the daily struggle of life and relationships. Sara Zavacki-Moore delivers a powerful narrative of hardship and loss leading to love and redemption. Prepare for a roller-coaster of emotion that will leave you with a whole new perspective on mental illness and the love we try to give to those who feel they don't deserve it."

~*Jennifer Peer, author of The Last Bloom*
~*~

"A story of sacrifice, self-discovery, and the search for love."

~*Joanne Brokaw, author of Suddenly Stardust*
~*~

"What follows is at times amusing, often profound, and generally reflective of feelings not often recognized or expressed. I was pulled in with the first sentence."

~*L. VanNostrand, M.S. in Child Development*

Dedication

To Matt—
You saw past my pain and believed in me
when I didn't have the strength to do so.
Thank you for everything.
You are still my favorite person.

Acknowledgements

I am grateful for all of the generous friends who helped me along this journey. Your time, encouragement and feedback have helped turn my dream into a reality. If I have forgotten to acknowledge anyone, please forgive me.

Thank you to Word Weavers of Western NY, Rachel E. Dewey, Andrew Wolf, Heather and Charlie Armstrong, Joanne Brokaw, Jenn Peer, Kristen Monro, and Joshua Miller.

L. VanNostrand and Rebecca Wolf, your countless hours providing me with feedback and input will never be forgotten. Thank you so much.

I would like to give a special thank you to my editor, Melanie Billings. Thank you for believing in me and helping me strengthen my writing. You played the biggest role in this show, and you deserve an encore. And of course thank you to my life partner and strongest supporter, Matthew Moore. To my children, Lydia and Malcolm, thank you for making me a mom. You are the best thing I have in life.

To all of the many clients, mental health professionals and colleagues I have had over the years, thank you for trusting me with your stories and insights. If mental illness plays a role in your story, just know that you are not alone. https://www.nami.org/help National Suicide Prevention Hotline 1-800-273-8255 https://suicidepreventionlifeline.org/

Chapter 1

Anxiety clung to Anna like sweat on a sultry day. Its familiar buzz radiated off her as she glanced at the clock on her dashboard.

Anna had good intentions. Really, she did. Leaving her monthly massage, she skipped her normal stop at the coffee shop so she could actually get to her therapist's on time. Today was her "wellness day," a phrase her therapist, Sheila, used *ad nauseam*. She also insisted on Anna calling her *Sheila* as a way of making them equals. Although, calling the therapist by her first name wasn't exactly helping Anna feel like they were in the same book, much less the same page. Therapy started a little less than a year ago, after Anna's first panic attack. At the time, she didn't know it was a panic attack; she thought for sure it was a heart attack. Before her episode, Anna had no idea a heart could beat so ridiculously fast. Her heart was so loud and rapid, she thought for sure she was dying. Catching her breath felt impossible. Even after puffing on her asthma inhaler, her chest felt squeezed tight, each breath fast and shallow. It was a memory she still felt in her body, the way her sweaty shirt clung to her back. Her thoughts swirling around her in a cloudy haze. It had been a rough year.

So, Anna sat in her car, contemplating all the things she didn't want to talk about in therapy. She reached over to the passenger seat and rubbed her fingers across the top of her leather-bound journal. Its etched cover design calmed her as she traced its indentations.

Traffic was slow. She was actually at a standstill when she happened to glance out the passenger side window. Getting stuck on any bridge, no matter how small, always made her feel a little panicky. She tried using what Sheila referred to as her "toolkit for anxiety" by taking some extra deep breaths. Closing her eyes for a few seconds, she idled behind a rusty pickup. Her tiny green hatchback purred as she sat nestled in the bucket seat. When she blinked her eyes open, she was relieved to see the buff construction guy ahead waving traffic forward. A few cars began to move while she impatiently idled.

Suddenly, the door of the pickup in front of Anna flung open, and a woman with long black hair tumbled out. A sharp yell rang out as the truck began to pull away. *Wait. What? Didn't anyone else notice her?* The woman stumbled across the pavement and threw herself up onto the curb. Anna watched, bewildered that all of the clueless drivers around her were bent toward the phones in their hands. Eyes haphazardly glanced up to move a pace, then back to their glowing addictions. The car behind Anna angrily beeped as she took her foot off the brake and eased forward into the stop-and-go flow of traffic. *What happened? Is she all right?* Glancing into the rearview mirror, she tried to catch a glimpse of her. All she could see was the impatient car behind her as the driver delivered hand gestures and expletives.

She continued driving straight for a moment but couldn't shake the thought of the woman. The truck was now long gone. Traffic was beginning to return to a normal pace. *What if she was hurt? Didn't anyone else see what happened? Someone must have called 911 by now.* Flipping on the turning signal, she turned right onto the next side street. Following it to the end and taking the next right, she hoped the next turn would bring her back up on the main street near the small bridge. It worked, and the woman was still there. Only instead of sitting on the curb, she was now pulling herself up onto the ledge of the bridge. A quick flash of black against the amber sunset, her knee-high boots shone dark against the pale whiteness of her legs.

Pulling her car up to the curb, she threw it into park. The woman's other foot stretched to the top of the ledge. Anna's mind raced as the woman shifted her weight, easing herself all the way up. The familiar onset of multiple thoughts flooded her brain. *This isn't a very high bridge. Is she trying to kill herself? Surely there are better bridges to choose from. Wait...what a horrible thought. Why isn't anyone else helping her? I can't be the only person who sees her teetering up there!* Anna glanced around to ask someone for help. A few pedestrians stood nearby, their phones masking their faces as they filmed their daily dose of drama.

Inky-black hair whipped in the wind as the woman stood with slumped shoulders looking over the edge. No one approached her to help.

Quickly, Anna pushed open the car door and began climbing out. A horn blasted as another car swerved past her. The air blew wisps of blonde hair into her face, temporarily blinding her. Sweeping it away from her eyes and securing her bangs with her sunglasses, she slammed the door shut and ran around the front of the car toward the woman. Seconds later, a large pickup sideswiped her car, taking the side mirror with it. Anna's heart raced as she paused and stared at the close call. Turning back toward the woman, she made her way over while watching her closely.

The sound of the crash must have made her turn. She lost her balance, slipping backward off the small ledge to safety. Her ankle twisted in a sickly manner as she crumpled into a sitting position on the damp pavement.

Crunching past a broken beer bottle, Anna rushed toward her. The heel of her favorite shoe catching on the edge of the curb. It snapped off and sent her flying. Anna's body careened toward the woman as she threw her arms out to buffer the space between them. Her hands involuntarily rose as she landed beside her on the cement. Her wrist smacked the pavement as she hit the ground. If the situation was different, it could have passed as a bad comedy routine.

Jet-black hair covered one side of the woman's face. Reaching up, she tucked it behind a generously pierced ear. Her glassy green gaze met Anna's, and she could see a lifetime of despair in her eyes.

"Okay, great. So you almost hit me with your car, and now you run over here to feel me up? And I don't even know your name," she quipped.

Is she trying to be funny? What is going on? Wasn't she just trying to jump off a bridge?

"Oh my gosh, no," Anna stammered. "I'm so sorry…I mean, no…what? I was actually trying to save you. I thought you were gonna jump!"

"So you crashed your car?"

"Well, actually, I didn't crash my car. Some idiot

side—I, I mean really, are you okay?" Anna paused and took a deep breath. Most of the cars had moved on. "I thought you were gonna jump. Are you okay? What happened with the truck back there? Can I call someone for you?" As Anna turned toward her car, she noticed her neck was already tightening up. Sheila would tell her to "breathe into the pain." But she knew it was only a matter of time before a migraine started. One of the perks of therapy was how she now had great insight into how stress exacerbated physical pain. If only she knew the secret of stopping it.

"There's no one to call," the woman said in a small voice.

They sat, side by side, bruised strangers past the confines of small talk.

"Well, at least let me call an ambulance. It seems like you hurt your ankle."

Anna waited until the woman nodded, then she eased herself off the ground. The familiar stab of pain shot down her neck as she walked to the passenger side of her car. Blindly rummaging around in her purse, she pushed aside old receipts and wrappers. Finally, she located her cell phone and dialed 911. Her explanation was as jumbled as her thoughts. Anna felt self-conscious listening to herself, aware of the panicky way her voice rose at the end of each sentence. Unsure of what else to do, she yanked her purse out of the car, walked back to the woman, and eased herself to the ground beside her. They sat in thick silence. Anna gently rubbed her wrist, aware of the bright bruise making an appearance.

The paramedics soon arrived, yet it felt as if they were in a time warp. Everything moved in slow motion.

A heavy-set state trooper scribbled on his forms. Concerned, friendly faces whispered, assessing bumps and bruises. As they prepared to load her into the ambulance, the woman grabbed her good hand and held on so hard her fingers started to tingle. Her grip seemed to beg for Anna to stay with her. She felt too bad to pull her hand away. The voices and colors seemed to fade as Anna replayed the last few minutes in her overwhelmed mind.

She struggled to climb into the ambulance with the stranger. An EMT held out his hand to assist, and she gratefully grabbed it. She pushed away the intrusive thought about how many germs were now on her hand, resisting the urge to pull the hand sanitizer from her purse.

The ride to the hospital was quiet, with the siren silenced. Each bump resonated down the length of her arthritic spine. She scrolled through her phone, trying to decide who to text about her car. Maybe she could take a taxi back to it from the hospital?

Squeezing the bridge of her nose, the beginning of a dreaded aura began creeping along her field of vision. Anna studied the interior of the ambulance, noting how everything was beginning to blur and shift. If she didn't take her migraine pill soon, she'd be hit with the pain and nausea, not to mention dealing with the repercussions of a migraine for days. Thankfully, she had thought to grab her purse. She felt around until her fingers located the pillbox. She pulled out the silver blister pack, peeled one open, and stuck the small white wafer onto her tongue. It dissolved into a milky blob as it slid down the back of her throat. The EMT watched in silence. Anna gave him a small smile, and he returned one. The woman beside her closed her eyes, and Anna watched her. Her dark tresses reminded her of the pond she used to swim in on hot summer nights in Maine. *How does she keep her hair so shiny?* She reached up to touch her own fair hair. *I should get my roots touched up.* The stranger felt for her hand again, found it, and squeezed. Her nails were short with remnants of black polish. A knotted Celtic ring encircled one finger. When Anna caught her looking, she turned away.

"By the way, I'm Anna. What's your name?" She turned back to her and whispered into her ear. The bumping in the back of the ambulance made speaking directly into her ear difficult.

The woman remained silent.

"Can I call someone for you?"

More silence.

"I know this sounds crazy," Anna continued. "Once we get there, I may never see you again. I want to make sure you're okay."

She turned toward Anna and whispered, "Why would you even care? Pretend you never met me. Forget this happened." Tears brightened her green eyes and slipped down her cheeks. "I don't need a savior." Letting go of Anna's hand, she angrily swiped the dampness away.

"What do you mean, 'forget it happened?' I can't *forget* it. I don't work that way. I want to help you." *This lady has some serious problems.*

The ambulance pulled up to the Emergency Department, and the doors opened. Before Anna could respond, EMTs removed the gurney from the back, and they wheeled the woman away. A gangly man in scrubs brought her in to get an X-ray. She sat and waited while they wrapped up her sprained wrist. Her foot was tapping the floor with lightning speed. Her jangled nerves couldn't keep up with her body.

Hospitals are fast and slow at the same time. Exhausted staff rushed around the space, reminding Anna of zombies suffering from mild panic attacks. While those sick or in pain impatiently stared at them in between glances at their phones. When her stomach rumbled, Anna became aware again of the throbbing between her eyes. If she didn't find some food fast, this would turn into a full-blown migraine, pill, or no pill.

A few minutes later, she sat clutching her vending machine specialty coffee with her good hand while waiting for the discharge paperwork. The cubby they offered consisted of a hard wooden bench, a wall hook, and a tattered magazine. As a germaphobe, she was determined to touch as little as possible. These places were microbiome factories. Her feet rested on top of a small heater that happened to be under the bench. Her lopsided shoes were unnoticed here. The warmth and hum of the heater made her suddenly drowsy. The space was somehow reminiscent of school bus rides. For a second, she saw herself as an awkward third grader. Memories of giggling with her best friend Elizabeth as they rested their feet on the wheel well filled her mind.

"Okay." A chubby nurse interrupted the memory as she clomped over. "Here's your paperwork. You're free to go."

"Oh, okay, thanks. You wouldn't happen to know where the woman who came in with me is?"

"I'm sorry," she replied. "I can't give out her

information. It's confidential."

Meeting the nurse's gaze, Anna cleared her throat. "I just wanted to make sure she's okay. If I don't at least get her number to check on her later, it will keep me awake tonight. You know what I mean?" She could feel her chest flooding with anxiety and tried to slow down her jumbled thoughts. Blowing out a slow breath, she continued, "I know it's against protocol, but couldn't you at least point me in her direction?" The nurse gave her a tight, small smile but remained silent.

Feeling dejected, Anna hung her head and sighed. Her neck was now so stiff it made it impossible to ignore the familiar ache moving down her shoulder and upper arm. Reaching back, she rubbed at the base of her skull, digging her knuckles into the trigger point there. *Why can't I be like other people? The kind of people who breeze through life, not allowing the stress of the moment to turn into physical symptoms?* The nurse held her hand out, motioning for Anna to return the paper. She scribbled something on the top and handed it back. Her shoes squeaked as she made her way down the sterile hallway. Reluctantly, Anna grabbed her coat and hobbled toward the door. Glancing down at the hospital paperwork, written in clear blue ink on the top of the paper, the nurse had scribbled, "*Kylie Teeter: Observation Status.*"

Part 1: Anna

Chapter 2

Anna

After catching a ride home, Anna changed and washed up the best she could with a bandaged wrist. Putting the kettle on for tea, she was desperate to calm her nerves. Chamomile wasn't quite soothing enough to quiet down her overactive brain. As was often the case, a pattern emerged from the random onslaught of thoughts. It became a mantra in her mind. *She isn't my problem. Not my responsibility. I don't even know her. She's probably not even there anymore.*

Dunking her tea bag into the steaming water, she allowed the thought loop to start again. *Not my problem. Not my responsibility. She's probably not even there anymore. Not my problem, not my responsibility.*

Sighing and setting her mug back down, she picked up her phone and hit the redial button for a rideshare.

Rush hour wasn't as bad as she thought it would be as they pulled back up to the hospital a short time later. Anna hoped her long-sleeve navy T-shirt would make the sling around her appear less conspicuous. It was already cutting into the delicate skin of her inner wrist. Rubbing the tender area again, she paused and gave the driver an extra twenty dollars. Turns out rideshare drivers have no problem sitting in their car while you run into the corner store. Thank God she spotted one along the way. Her mother's investment in Miss Manners Summer Camp paid off. Anna smiled. *I may have some problems, but manners isn't one of them. Never visit someone in the hospital empty-handed.* Anna could hear this new mantra repeating in her head along with *Not my problem. Not my responsibility.*

A warm spring breeze blew her bangs across her forehead. She missed her long hair. Pulling the patchwork bag over her still tight shoulder, she slammed the car door and made her way toward the entrance. Her heart thumped as she walked through the lobby. Anxiety had a way of permeating every aspect of her day. The overly sweet aroma of flavored coffee filled the air as her stomach swirled with nervous energy.

This is ridiculous. I feel like I'm doing something wrong. Sweeping her still damp hair behind one ear, she began fiddling with an earring. Passing the pastry cart, she followed the red line down the hallway floor leading to the elevator. Inside the claustrophobic space, a young mother sat in a wheelchair holding a tiny newborn swaddled in pink. Gripping the handles behind her, a man bent over them. His spindly fingers reached out to stroke the pink petal cheek of his daughter. He beamed as he smiled up at Anna.

"Can you believe I left the car seat up in the room? It's a good thing we realized it before we got to the car!" Anna smiled at them as the bell rang, and they exited. Now alone in the elevator, she watched the numbers light up, marking the way down to the emergency room. As she stepped onto the unit, her gaze settled on the large sign on the wall. The hallway echoed each step as she approached *Pre-admission/Observation.* Stopping at the large glass window, she leaned in to speak.

"Excuse me. I'm looking for Kylie Teeter. She was brought in about two hours ago? In observation? Do you know if she is still here?" She winced at the inflection of her own squeaky voice.

"Two hours? Yeah, if it's only been two hours, she's probably still here. Are you family?" The receptionist's fingers flew across her keyboard as she stared at her computer monitor.

"Um…no, I came in with her. There was a kind of, um, accident?"

The woman tapped on the glass, cutting her off.

"Hold on." She typed something into the keyboard. "She's still here." She clicked another button on the screen. "She's stable." She paused, staring at Anna as if she was hoping she would walk away. When she didn't, the woman sighed, setting down a patient's chart and scooching her chair closer to the computer monitor.

"What's your name? I'll see if she can have a visitor."

"Anna Johnson."

She popped off her chair and disappeared around the corner.

Anna felt ridiculous as she stood rubbing her wrapped wrist while her bag slid down her other arm. It felt like she was back in Girl Scouts, having to wait on some stranger's front steps while they grabbed spare change and crushed dollar bills. Soft tones came from the hallway as the lady returned.

"Follow me." She led her down a fluorescently lit hallway lined with empty hospital beds and wheelchairs.

"In there." Pointing at an ugly multi-colored curtain, she turned and walked away.

Trying to calm her breathing, Anna paused outside of the outdated pastel print.

"Suicide watch."

"What?" Her eyes widened as she peeked around the corner of the curtain. The crumpled woman on the bed repeated herself.

"I'm on suicide watch, hence Officer Krupke." She raised a hand in the direction of the rotund man sitting near the edge of the small cubical-like space.

"I told you, I'm not a police officer. I'm security. Just here to keep an eye on you." The man raised his eyes from his newspaper and gave a tight smile.

"Oh, I'm sorry...I mean, maybe this is a bad time?" Anna's palms were now covered in sweat as she clutched her bag.

"A bad time?" Kylie snorted. "Is there really a good time for something like this?"

Standing there, Anna began twisting the back of her earring while regarding the woman who somehow appeared younger than she had a few hours ago. Her hospital gown clung to bony shoulders, revealing how slender she was. Her bright green eyes were lined with thick smudges of black mascara. A smattering of freckles danced across her nose.

"Sit down," Kylie directed. "Please," she whispered.

Grabbing a chair from alongside the officer, Anna pulled it toward the bed. It scraped along the linoleum as she struggled to keep the bag from sliding all the way down her arm. *Can this be any more awkward?* Giving up, she carefully set the bag on the floor.

"How did you find me?"

"Oh, um, a nurse sort of led me in your direction."

Kylie picked at the pages of the magazine on her bed. An awkward silence hung in the air.

"I wanted to see if you were okay," Anna said while reaching down into the bag. "Um, actually, I brought you something." She gingerly pulled out a prickled green plant encased in cellophane. Dirt clung to the plastic.

"A cactus? Interesting choice." Kylie smirked.

"I know it's a bit strange. It seemed appropriate."

"How so?"

"It blooms in the midst of unlivable conditions."

"Hmm, what, are you a philosopher, or do you specialize in plants?" Kylie snorted.

"No, I'm just a hairdresser."

"Just? Don't say 'just.' Hairdressers are vital in this society," Kylie said while absently touching her hair. "I mean, I usually look better than this." She chuckled and gave Anna a grin. "Um, thank you for the plant."

"You're welcome." It felt like she had a stale piece of bread lodged in her throat. "So, when do you get to go home?"

"As soon as they decide I won't try to off-myself again. They want me to meet with a shrink this afternoon. Then they'll tell me if I can go. They need the bed—ya know? No room for you unless you jump and somehow survive." She paused as she noticed Anna's surprise at her candor.

"Sorry, I tend to either make stupid remarks or talk

non-stop when I'm nervous," Kylie said.

"It's okay. I didn't mean to make you nervous. Maybe I should go. I felt like I needed to come back and make sure you were okay." Anna bent to retrieve her bag. She forgot it would be lighter now that the plant was gone.

"I'm okay," she whispered. "But you can stay awhile if you want to."

****

Forty-five minutes passed before Anna felt like she could justify leaving the room. She tried to make conversation, but Kylie's one-word responses made it difficult. Finally, the officer stood up and handed Anna the glossy magazine he'd been thumbing through. Flipping through the pages, she could feel her stomach rumbling. A loud gurgle escaped, and she cleared her throat, hoping Kylie wouldn't notice.

Sprawled on the hospital bed, Kylie continued to scroll through her phone. The silence in the room amplified the one-sided discussion Anna's stomach was having. When Kylie made a snide joke about it, she decided to excuse herself to go to the cafeteria.

Following the signs back to the elevators, she took one to the basement. Expecting a dim and dank area, she was surprised when the elevator doors opened to a bright and colorful room. A variety of smells greeted her, and her stomach responded with another gurgle. The antiseptic scent of bleach and bandages from upstairs was replaced by the tantalizing smells of steaming vegetables, mac and cheese, and baked chicken. Warm water droplets clung to the back of the stacked trays. Lifting one and gripping the sides, she followed the line toward the hot food. It was surprising to see a large pot of homemade mac and cheese, complete with crumbled crackers on top. A tiny woman with huge hair stuck a slotted metal spoon into it. Her hair was stark white and poofed out in all directions. A black hairnet strained to keep it in place. Her smile was as expansive as her hair.

"Good afternoon! What a lovely day it is. Would you like some pasta, dear?" Her southern drawl was charming. *So much for eating healthy today.*

"Yes, please." Anna held her tray up to the woman, who placed a heaping spoonful of the food onto the plate. Continuing down the line, she bypassed the steaming pot of peas and paused at the apple crisp. *Might as well. It's not like I have any men to lose weight for.*

After paying, she walked over to an empty table and ate her meal in silence while scrolling through her phone, pretending she didn't feel uncomfortable. The din of conversations around her taking her back to her elementary lunchroom. She recalled the awkward feeling of isolation settling beneath the hunger. Anna was surprised to see an email from her pastor. Seeing as she hadn't been to church in ages, she was curious to see what it contained. Hoping for a personalized message from him, she was disappointed to see it was a newsletter and a sign-up for a fundraiser. Anna grew up in the church but left the prison of her ultra-evangelical background when she turned eighteen. Now it seemed as if she was working out any religious guilt with her sporadic attendance to a local non-denominational church. Yet, despite her purposefully limited relationship with God, she often found her childhood convictions still shaped many of her everyday decisions.

Is that why I'm here? Am I supposed to help this woman somehow? The fluttering in her heart gave her the answer she sought. God or no God, Anna's ongoing fear of hellfire and brimstone prompted her to be as helpful to humanity as possible.

By the time she returned to the room, Kylie was gone. The sheets lay in a crumpled heap.

"She'll be back." The officer picked up a steaming cup of coffee and blew across the top of it. "They took her to a psych eval. You might as well go for a walk or something. I'm told she'll be gone for at least another hour."

"Oh. Okay. Thanks."

By the time Anna reached the hospital lobby, it was raining. Pausing to watch the droplets of water clinging to the expansive wall of windows, she considered her options. Would leaving now seem super rude? After all, she'd done her duty by coming out here and checking in on Kylie. It would be easy to slip out and never see her again. Yet, never seeing her again somehow seemed *wrong*. For reasons she couldn't quite understand, she turned and walked into the hospital gift shop, hoping to kill some more time. After all, she'd written her cellphone number on a small piece of paper and left it with a note on Kylie's bed. *Not my problem. Not my responsibility,* her brain reminded her. While gazing at the rack of gourmet chocolates, her phone buzzed.

—*Hey, cactus lady, I'm back.*—

****

Back in Kylie's cubby, the curtain now stood open, and the police officer was gone.

Anna searched for something to keep herself busy and began folding the worn hospital blanket. The edge of the covering was unraveling on one side. Folding the tattered part into the middle, so it wouldn't show, she smoothed the fabric. "So, you said they are finishing some paperwork and sending you to a women's shelter?" Kylie had barely spoken since Anna returned. Apparently, during her trip to the gift shop, the staff decided Kylie no longer needed to be here. This seemed a bit short-sighted to Anna.

"Unfortunately, there are men there too," Kylie quipped. Anna glanced at her to see if she was joking. She was still trying to get used to Kylie's odd sense of humor.

"Wait, I don't understand—why can't you go home?"

"I don't exactly have a *home* anymore." Kylie smiled wearily and paused before explaining. "I was staying with this guy…and let's just say I'm not quite welcome there anymore."

Anna didn't push the issue any further. Kylie's unfortunate exit from the pickup truck explained a lot. She reminded herself she didn't even know this woman, and her life wasn't any of her business. Kylie was like a small, wounded bird trying its hardest to fly away despite how much it hurt.

"Are they making you go to this shelter as part of your…I don't know, some sort of *safety* plan?"

"No." Kylie hobbled to the faux wood armoire and pulled out the bright turquoise plastic bag holding her shoes and clothing. "But they have to get rid of me and have to make sure I have someplace to sleep tonight. After that, I'm no longer their problem."

As she stood gazing out the window, a slight chill swept over Anna despite the sweltering heat of the room. *Everything in life happens for a reason.*

"Stay with me." The words popped out of her mouth before she could filter or judge them. It felt strangely freeing for a few seconds before the self-judgment crept in. *Did I really just invite a stranger to live with me? What am I doing? Am I going to regret this later? What happened to not my problem, not my responsibility?* She could feel her body manifesting her anxiety as another familiar ache seized her neck.

"Huh?" Kylie dropped the bag back onto the bed. "You don't even know me. You're gonna let a complete stranger stay at your house? Didn't your mom teach you about stranger danger?"

"You're not a *complete* stranger. I know this is gonna sound bizarre, but I actually have an ad online to look for a roommate. And so far, the handful of people I've interviewed have been less than desirable. I really do need a roommate, and you need a room—right?"

Kylie stared at her as she picked at the ragged edge of a cuticle. An overhead announcement broke the silence. The nasally voice stated all hospital discharges were to wait in their rooms for their corresponding paperwork.

Clearing her throat, Anna looked directly at Kylie. "I'm not saying it's permanent. I mean, if it doesn't work out, or you don't pay the rent or something, I will have to ask you to leave, but…"

A sob escaped Kylie's throat. "You would do that for me?"

"Why not?" Anna replied, ignoring the doubts piling up in her mind. She smiled as the nurse entered the room with her arms full of papers.

****

Along the route home, silence permeated the car, interspersed with small pleasantries. Although she didn't act outwardly hostile, Kylie gave Anna the impression she didn't want to talk. When Anna asked her about stopping by her old place for more clothes and personal items, Kylie turned to stare out her window and quickly replied, "I can't go back there." Then she laid her head against the car window and closed her eyes. Anna's curiosity was piqued, but she felt like if she asked too many questions, she'd scare her into more silence.

So she stopped asking and kept her eyes on the road as they approached her cozy tree-lined neighborhood. There was a small lunch crowd gathering at the café on the corner of the street.

Easing the car onto the crumbling driveway, Anna turned and smiled.

"Here we are. Home sweet home."

The gaping asphalt was the least of Anna's problems. Two overgrown trees drooped sadly in the front yard. The grass grew in spotty patches, with bright yellow dandelions sprinkled throughout. Cheap plywood adorned the front door where the window used to be. Kylie remained silent as she took in the whole scene.

"I know things are a bit run down. I've been really busy at work, and money has been pretty tight." Anna sighed.

"How long exactly have you been searching for a roommate?"

"A while. Sorry, like I said, money has been tight. I

was planning on putting the house up for sale if I didn't find someone by the end of the month. My last roommate…didn't work out." Anna grabbed Kylie's plastic hospital bag and opened the car door.

"Come on in, and I'll show you around." She unlocked the door while Kylie hobbled up the front step and into the entryway. A small wooden table sat in the corner by the door. Anna noticed that Kylie's gaze drifted to the bright red ceramic bowl on top of the table. The bowl was quite intricate and consisted of different shades of red glass beads. Tiny blue-flowered tiles circled its opening. It was reminiscent of a Frida Kahlo painting.

"What a beautiful piece," Kylie said. "Did you make it?"

"No, I wish. My grandmother made it. She learned how to make them in Austria when she was little. She gave it to me when I turned sixteen." Nana Jo always kept her favorite candy in it. *No matter how many pieces of chocolate I ate, it was always magically replenished.* Carefully placing her keys in the bowl, Anna led Kylie down the hall.

"So this is the room. I forgot to tell you it is fully furnished. I guess it's your lucky day." Anna regretted the words as soon as they exited her mouth. *Has Kylie ever had any good luck in her life?*

"Is there a bus line here?" Kylie asked. "I have to go back to work next Monday. I should have thought to ask about the bus line."

"Of course. The stop is actually at the corner."

Anna thought for a moment before continuing. "I have to go shopping this afternoon. Do you want to come with me to pick up some things for yourself?"

"That would be great. But if it's easier for you, I can take the bus."

"Don't be crazy. I'm going out anyway."

****

The next few days were a bit of a blur as Anna adjusted to Kylie's presence in the house. Despite the running commentary of obsessive thoughts in her head, Anna kept trying to remind herself that she hadn't made a mistake in inviting Kylie to live with her. Now she seemed to be stuck in a migraine cycle. The pain in her head was the first thing she thought of upon waking, and recently just getting through the day was overwhelming her. Last night was especially difficult. By the time she finished washing up the dinner dishes, her vision was getting blurry. She washed her sleeping pill down with her final swig of wine. The throbbing in her head was so painful that she could feel it in her teeth. Finally around eight p.m., she allowed herself to climb into bed with a heat pack. The sweet oblivion of sleep offering her a brief respite from the pain.

****

Walking into Sheila's office always put Anna at ease. Even the very first time she arrived for therapy, her anxiety quieted as she stepped into the room. The walls were a pale blue, and the dim lighting gave the space a calming atmosphere. Both windows were large, with white lace curtains pulled aside, allowing for a view of the field behind the office building. The window shades were tucked up but could be pulled down for more privacy if needed.

The field outside was untended but still beautiful. Long grass, interspersed with Queen Anne's lace and various other dainty weeds, created a haven for butterflies and crickets. The low hum of the crickets' song often filled the spaces between Anna's conversation with Sheila.

Today, Sheila wore her typical long skirt and peasant blouse. If she were a decade older, she would have been a flower child. Her silver bracelets clinked against each other as she held out her hand to greet Anna.

"How are you today?" she asked, motioning to the puffy chair.

Wincing slightly as she sat, Anna replied, "I'm all right. Stressed, but that's pretty normal for me."

"And your level of pain?" Sheila asked.

"Um." Anna paused to think before answering. Technically, she was supposed to describe her daily physical pain as discomfort. This apparently took some of the power away from the demon that had plagued her for the past several years. "It's been a rough week. I've had a migraine since yesterday, and my lower back is acting up."

"I'm sorry to hear that. It sounds like you're dealing with some extra stress, and this is affecting your physical symptoms."

Anna nodded.

"What would you say has been the biggest stressor this week for you?"

Picking up her water, Anna took a long sip. "It's kind of a crazy story."

Sheila raised her eyebrows but remained silent.

"So, last week I met this woman, Kylie. She was, and I know how crazy this sounds, but she was standing on this ledge near the overpass, and I tried to pull over to see if she was all right."

She studied Sheila's face for any sign of judgment. Finding none, she continued. "We started talking, I called an ambulance, and we rode to the hospital together. Later, when she was ready to leave the hospital and didn't have anywhere to go, I, um, I basically invited her to move in with me."

"Hmmm," Sheila began. "I'm not sure I'm understanding correctly. This woman, Kylie, went to the hospital after trying to jump from the overpass, and you invited her to live with you?"

"I know, I know, it sounds ridiculous. But her eyes seemed so very sad. She didn't have anywhere to go."

Sheila nodded for her to continue.

"And I have been looking for a housemate anyway…"

"Yes?"

"You think it was dumb of me, right? Do you think I made a mistake? I mean, I know she is a complete stranger, but I felt compelled to help her. Almost like she was put in my path for a reason."

"It sounds like she was in a desperate situation. I am a bit surprised the hospital didn't keep her longer. Did they connect her up with mental health services?"

"Oh, yeah. I mean, I guess she has a therapist and is on some medication. I don't really know all of the details. Do you think I should have minded my own business?"

"I think you saw an individual who was in trouble, and you decided to help."

Anna nodded. Why did she always revert to feeling guilty about everything in her life?

"I'm wondering if your decision to become involved with this woman is related at all to your need to feel wanted or perhaps, needed?"

"I know." They had talked about her constant role as a caregiver throughout her life. It started as a child with her parents and continued into adulthood.

"And," Shelia continued, "in the past when you've taken on that role, your negative physical symptoms have increased."

"Yeah. I see the pattern. But, with Henry, it was different. I mean, when he got sick, what was I supposed to do, leave? *Not* help because it would make my pain worse?"

"I'm not saying that at all. I guess I'm wondering about your need to feel needed? Do you have any friends in your life who enjoy spending time with you without needing something from you in return?"

The crickets' gentle chorus filled the air.

Anna took another sip of water. "Well, yeah. I mean, most of my friends don't seem too needy to me. But I like helping them." She paused.

"Okay, I hear what you're saying. You're right," Anna admitted. "I know a lot of my self-worth is based on how much other people need me. Aren't we supposed to help other people in need? I can't go through life ignoring other people's needs, just because it affects my health, can I?"

She held her therapist's gaze.

"It sounds like you are aware of this pattern, and it's important to you to help others?" Sheila said.

"Yeah," said Anna. "Of course it's important." Sometimes she felt super annoyed with Sheila, but rather than admit her frustration and come across as rude, she swallowed it down and ignored it.

Chapter 3

Kylie

Feeling as worn out as an old leather purse, Kylie stumbled into the breezeway, following Anna. Even though they'd already eaten lunch, they stopped for some appetizers at a small Mexican restaurant next door to the grocery store. The restaurant was a favorite of Anna's, one she used to frequent often. Now, their stomachs were full and their wallets empty.

Kylie stood in the entranceway, not wanting to appear too comfortable in her new home. She followed Anna into the kitchen with the bags of groceries and started to put the items away.

"Oh, it's okay. I can take care of this. Why don't you go and lie down? You must be pretty tired." Anna motioned toward Kylie's new room. "There are fresh linens in your closet, so help yourself to anything you need."

Kylie was too tired to resort to a smart remark, so she thumped down the dim hallway and eased her bedroom door closed. Sinking onto the pillow-strewn bed, she drifted to sleep.

Someone was chasing her. The dank hallway continued from building to building. The only light was from the flickering candles lining the walls. She ran faster and faster, and just as she thought she was getting ahead, she felt the warmth of breath on her neck. Her lungs ached. The black-and-white checkered interior of the hall terrified her. Its patterns warped like a demented funhouse. A small light shone in the distance. The breathing behind her grew louder. She closed her eyes and lunged forward.

Kylie woke with a start. Sweat matted her hair. She shivered and sat up. The odor in the room sickened her. It was perspiration mixed with fear, like a Catholic school gym locker room. Swinging her legs over the side of the bed, she eased her way up and hobbled over to the closet. The light clicked on as soon as she opened the door, forcing her to blink away any remnants of sleep. She gazed in wonder at the items before her. Boxes of unopened linens lined the shelves. *What in the world? There must be ten sets of sheets here. Who needs all these sheets?*

She glanced at the other side of the closet, which was empty except for a set of towels with matching washcloths. Grabbing the set, she shut the door and headed toward the bathroom. Along the way, she scooped up her makeup bag and set it onto the tiled floor. *This is amazing.* Thinking back on her last bathroom, she shuddered. No matter how hard she tried, she could never keep it clean. After a while, she gave up trying. When you had to share a bathroom with men, you learned to stop caring. This bathroom had cracks in the tile and a drippy faucet, but it was clean. Turning on the water to the tub, she grabbed the plastic bag she carried in with her and tied it over her cast. Cognizant of her leg, she climbed in. *Might as well mark my territory.* With a steady hand, she lifted the small zippered bag from the floor and sighed.

****

"Hey, did you get some sleep?" Anna asked. She was already dressed for the day. Her thin blonde hair was pulled into a messy bun, yet she still managed to convey elegance in her jeans and white T-shirt. She pulled some freshly baked chocolate chip cookies out of the oven. Kylie inhaled with a dramatic flair and smiled as she sat down at the table.

She couldn't remember the last time she ate anything that didn't come from a can or a box.

"I already ate dinner, but I saved you some soup in the fridge if you want to warm it up. The cookies should be cool in a few minutes, and then you can help yourself."

"You don't have to cook for me."

"Oh, don't worry. I don't cook very often. But I made a big pot of soup, so there is plenty for both of us. I had a chocolate craving, and I couldn't resist baking cookies. Once you get settled a bit more, you can stock your own supply of food. I made some room for you in the fridge."

Kylie cracked open the door. "I don't think I'll fit."

Anna laughed. "You're funny. My last roommate wasn't so funny." She paused for a moment. "So, where do you work?" Anna grabbed a spatula and began lifting the cookies from the pan.

Kylie grabbed a cookie and shoved it in her mouth. A rush of heat hit her throat, and the chocolate oozed over her singed tongue.

"I'm a stripper," Kylie said with a grin and grabbed another cookie, popping it into her mouth.

"You're kidding, right?"

"Nope. Not kidding. Are you gonna kick me out

now?"

"Of course not; I don't know when to take you seriously. Are you really a stripper?" Anna's face bore the expression of a child watching a calf being born at the state fair. "I mean, I guess I've never met a stripper before."

"Well, we are real live people too," Kylie retorted. "You're not a born-again-gonna-preach-at-me-type, are you?" Kylie narrowed her eyes and sat up straighter in the chair.

"I believe in God if that's what you're asking. But I'm not so much into preaching to people. Judging them either." Anna put another cookie on Kylie's plate and turned toward the cupboard. "Want some milk?"

"Sure."

Anna grabbed a glass from the cupboard before Kylie managed to open the refrigerator door.

"You don't have to serve me, ya know." Kylie's voice was muffled as she poked her head into the refrigerator.

"I know." Pouring them each a tall glass, she settled back down on the chair. Kylie squirmed a bit under her watchful gaze. She prepared herself to answer nosy questions about her chosen profession.

"So"—Anna slid the plate of cookies closer—"do you have to work tonight?"

"No."

"Wanna watch a movie with me? I have one of those streaming movie apps."

Kylie smiled and followed her into the living room.

****

Before she left for work the next evening, Kylie inspected herself in the mirror. She wore one of her black leather boots and the ugly plastic boot the hospital gave her for her ankle. There was no way she could walk without it. The plastic was thick and black, with a hefty black piece of Velcro holding the cast in place. Her denim skirt grazed her upper thighs, and her skintight tank top revealed a variety of colorful tattoos on each of her shoulders. The right shoulder bore a bouquet of flowers, with vines creeping around her upper arm. The other shoulder was an evening sky, complete with a large white moon over a deep blue twilight. A smattering of yellow stars encircled it.

"My boss is gonna kill me," Kylie said as she slung her purse over her shoulder. "I told him I was in an accident and couldn't dance, but he doesn't know about this stupid cast. He said I could bartend for a few weeks until I can get back on stage."

Anna paused and regarded her, then asked, "Why don't you look for a different job? I mean, I'm not trying to judge you. I just…"

"Wish I did something more respectable?" Kylie raised her eyebrows. "I make good money. Who cares that men lust after me? They do it whether you have clothes on or not, Anna. Didn't you know that? Men are pigs. All they want is to size you up and lay you down. I might as well get paid for it." Kylie abruptly grabbed her house key and slammed the door behind her.

Anna watched her hobble down the driveway toward the bus stop. What was that all about?

Chapter 4

Anna

She heard the door click open early the next morning. Glancing at her clock, she saw it was a few minutes past four a.m. It would take time to get used to sleeping through Kylie's schedule. She pulled the covers up tighter around her shoulders and soon fell back asleep.

Anna's eyes flew open. She heard a clunk. *What's going on? What time is it? My gosh! How is it seven already? I feel like I just closed my eyes.* There it was again. Anna grabbed her worn fleece robe and headed down the hall. A sudden piercing scream filled the space.

"Kylie? What's wrong?" Anna rushed into her room. Kylie's body thrashed against the wall beside her bed. Her fists were tight, and her hair slick with sweat.

"Kylie, wake up. You're having a bad dream. Kylie, wake up!"

She reached out and placed her hand on Kylie's arm, surprised that it was cold and clammy. Kylie flinched in her sleep, suddenly swinging her fist up and hitting Anna. Anna stumbled backward and caught herself by grabbing onto the comforter at the edge of the bed. She blinked in surprise, rubbing her jaw.

"What the? Ouch!" Anna shouted.

By that time, Kylie was sitting up, staring at Anna, her gaze liquid with disbelief.

Kylie gasped. "What happened? Did I hit you?"

Anna rubbed her wounded jaw.

"More like sucker-punched me. Geez, Kylie, what were you dreaming about?"

"Oh my God, I'm so sorry!" Kylie rubbed her knuckles and climbed out of bed. "Let me get you some ice. It's already starting to swell."

Anna sat down on the bed and gingerly touched her face. She could hear Kylie scurrying around the kitchen, searching for something to put the ice into. It would be easier to get it herself, but somehow, she simply didn't have the energy. Sighing, she glanced over at the dresser where Kylie's purse was lying half-open. A semi-crushed box of cigarettes spilled out onto the dresser. Inside the box, two cigarettes remained with a small roll of bills.

"Here you go. I'm so sorry." Kylie rushed over and handed her some ice cubes wrapped in a decorative kitchen towel.

"No, it's okay. I mean, I woke you up. It's not like you did it on purpose."

"I'm so sorry. Is it bad? I've never punched a girl...I...I hope it doesn't swell too much." Kylie walked over to the dresser and zipped up her purse.

"It will be fine. What were you dreaming about?" Anna asked.

"Huh? Oh, who knows?" Kylie chuckled and grabbed some stray socks left on the floor. She opened the top dresser drawer and shoved them inside. Anna took that as a cue to go.

"I'm really sorry. Um, I think I'll take a shower

before I go to work."

Kylie pulled the same drawer open again and rummaged around inside of it.

Anna stood and walked into the hallway. *Well, that was abrupt; guess we're done talking.*

"Okay. See ya later," Kylie said as she closed the bedroom door.

****

By the end of the workday, the right side of Anna's jaw was beginning to turn a sickly shade of blue. She winced at her reflection in one of the many mirrors.

"Honey, are you okay?" asked Helen, one of her favorite customers. She was eighty-three years old and came to the Snip and Shape Hair Salon and Spa every week to get her hair set. Helen had wiry white hair and watery blue eyes. Her voice was low and gravelly from years of smoking. Her wrinkled hands were as soft as silk. She loved Anna, and Anna dreaded the day Helen didn't show up for her set-and-dry.

"If a boy did this to you, dearie, you get up and get out! Do you hear me?" She grabbed Anna's hands and looked her in the eye. "I mean it. No boy is worth getting hurt over!"

Anna laughed. "No, Helen, I would never be with someone like that. It wasn't a boy. It was actually an accident. My roommate did it by accident."

Helen eyed her with suspicion. "You found a roommate?" She sat down at Anna's station. "So, you won't have to sell the house and move in with me after all?"

"No. I get to keep the house. At least for now," Anna replied with a smile.

"Thank the Lord Almighty, sweetheart. Because I

haven't had to share a house in thirty years!"

Anna laughed again and grabbed the blow dryer.

"Can I ask you a question, Helen?"

"Of course, my dear." Helen grabbed a piece of nicotine gum and shoved it in her mouth.

"Do you think it's a bad thing to care too much about people?" asked Anna.

"What do you mean, dear?"

"I dunno. I mean…do you think that if you care too much for other people, you are letting them walk all over you?"

"Are you talking about this new roommate of yours?" Helen took a bright red tube of lipstick from her purse and applied it with vigor.

"I seem to pick up strays? Ya know?"

"Honey, caring for people is a risk we take in life. It can hurt, but it can also be worth it. When I took care of my Johnny before the cancer got the best of him, I accepted some advice. A nurse told me if I didn't take better care of myself, I wouldn't be around to take care of him when he needed me the most. She was right. I was running myself ragged, trying to do everything for him. It took me way too long to realize I needed help. I got my friend to stay with him for two hours every Wednesday so I could take a break. It was good advice. Do you need a break, Anna? Is this one sick, too?"

Anna grabbed the hairspray. "No, not sick. But she needs something. Something I don't think I can give her.

"No one said you need to save them all, honey," Helen replied.

****

As Anna opened the front door and let herself in,

she could smell an overwhelming sweetness. A huge bouquet of yellow roses sat on her dining room table. She walked over and reached for the small note tucked near an outer stem.

—Anna, bet ya didn't bargain to let a mess like me walk into your life. You probably regret offering to let me stay here. I'm sorry I hit you. I'll be back in a few days. There is something I have to take care of. Kylie—

Anna bent to smell the sunny display. Her fingers stroked a petal. *Where did she go? What does she have to take care of? Something is strange here.* Glancing around as if she was being watched, Anna eased down the hallway. She opened Kylie's door, not sure what she was even looking for. The room was tidy. Anna's grandmother's quilt dressed up the bed nicely and gave it an inviting and cozy atmosphere. The lacy white curtains were open, and sunlight streamed into the quiet room. Anna gulped as she realized she'd only been in this room twice this past year. The first time was right after she got back from the hospital. The second time she went in to clean the room and remove all the memories.

Anna walked to the pine chest at the foot of the bed. Her grandmother's quilt had been kept there until Kylie found it and placed it on the bed.

It's just as well. It was meant to be used.

Anna lifted the heavy lid, feeling its smooth surface. She inhaled the familiar and pleasant aroma of cedar. It reminded her of her childhood. Her grandfather built a walk-in cedar closet for her grandmother years ago, and she and her cousins used to play in it. She placed her hand on top of the rose-patterned sheets folded in the corner. She remembered how she'd posted online that she needed extra sheets when Henry first got sick. Within two days, a handful of friends had dropped off several sets. Somehow she just never had the energy to return any of them. As she moved to close the box, she noticed a slight lump under the stack of sheets. Lifting the corner, she pulled out a small zipped bag. Perhaps it was a makeup or a pencil bag? Anna looked around, feeling guilty. She sat, pulling it onto her lap, surprised at how light it was. She felt like a kid caught with her hand in the cookie jar. An overwhelming temptation to slide the zipper and peek inside washed over her. Falling into the familiar role of a "good child," she resisted and tucked the bag back under the sheets.

"It's none of my business anyway," said Anna aloud. She smoothed the sheets down, reminding herself she was doing the right thing. Closing the chest with care, she walked away.

****

During the next five days of Kylie's absence, Anna continued to feel overwhelmed with curiosity. On two separate occasions, she found herself standing at the foot of Kylie's bed, staring at the chest. She resisted the urge to open it, despite the magnetic field it exuded.

Kylie blew back in several days later on Saturday as if she'd never been gone. Her keys jangled in the lock, and she threw open the door with such force it smashed into the wall behind it. The red bowl on the side table shook precariously.

"Hey, I got us a pizza," Kylie said as she motioned for Anna to grab the box.

"Pizza? I haven't even had breakfast yet." Anna grabbed the box and set it on the counter. "Where did you get fresh pizza so early in the morning?"

"I know a guy." Kylie snorted.

Anna shrugged and grabbed two plates from the cupboard. By the time she turned back around, Kylie was already shoving a greasy piece into her mouth. Anna hesitated for a moment before she grabbed a slice and set it on her plate. Should she ask Kylie where she went? Would she be prying too much if she did? She decided to take her chances.

"Did you get whatever you needed to do, done?"

"Huh? Oh, yeah. Sure, I guess," Kylie replied.

Before Anna could press any further, Kylie grabbed another slice and headed down the hallway.

Anna dumped her now soggy cereal into the sink and flipped the switch for the disposal. She took a swig of her coffee and grabbed her cell phone and keys. *If my mom was around to talk to, she'd know what to do. It's not like I can talk to Dad either. He thinks I'm his dead sister, Audrey. He's convinced it's 1972.* She set down the keys and phone and opened up her laptop. Her fingers froze over the keys. *What do I search for anyway? Crazy roommates with secrets? Geez, that sounds a bit like a Lifetime special."*

"Ugh!" she moaned. She closed the lid, grabbed her keys, and headed out the door.

Chapter 5

Anna

Kylie stayed in bed for the next two days. On the morning of the third day, Anna knocked again. This time when Kylie moaned, "Leave me alone," Anna opened the door and stepped inside. A putrid smell wafted through the room. It smelled like sweat and desperation, taking her momentarily back to her first middle school dance. The dim light peeked through the semi-closed curtains illuminated by the dust particles floating throughout the room.

"Get up," said Anna. Silence permeated the air. "Kylie, I mean it. This is ridiculous. You can't keep staying in bed. Are you sick? Don't you have to go to work?"

"Leave me alone. I told you yesterday, and I'm telling you again today. I'm fine. I'm tired. Leave me alone."

"No."

Anna opened the curtains to let in the light. Kylie responded by pulling the quilt over her mop of oily hair. Anna sighed and reached for the quilt. As she pulled it back, she gasped in horror.

"Kylie! What is this? Blood? Kylie! What did you do?"

"It's nothing. It's fine. Just a few nicks here and

there," she muttered. She tried to pull the quilt back up but gave up after realizing Anna still had a hold of it.

The blood wasn't fresh. At least a dozen brown spots smattered the sheets. Anna searched for the source of the injury. She grabbed Kylie's phone off the nightstand and dialed 911. While giving the operator her address, Anna peeled back the rest of the sheets and blankets. Kylie moaned. Her eyes were glazed and her cheeks flushed. She surprised Anna by allowing her to continue her search. Kylie's arms were bare and unblemished, except for the colorful tattoos. After noticing a small bloodstain on Kylie's nightshirt, Anna gingerly lifted it and exposed her stomach. Kylie's thighs and abdomen were covered with small cuts. They didn't appear too deep, and none were still bleeding. Two larger cuts, both on her stomach, were surrounded by deep pink. They looked like they could be infected. An empty prescription bottle sat open on the nightstand. Next to it, Anna recognized the small zippered bag. Its contents spilled out onto the bedside table. White gauze, a few Band-Aids, tweezers, a razor, and a tiny tube of ointment lay nearby. Anna studied Kylie for an explanation, but her eyes remained closed. Her cheeks pink with fever. Sighing, she sat on the bed beside her and waited for the ambulance.

****

Anna sat on the ugly plaid chair inside the observation unit of the hospital's psychiatric ward. She glanced up from her phone as a woman in dangerously high heels clicked her way into the room. Anna was somehow not surprised when the woman broke the silence with a syrupy sweet voice.

"Hello, Kylie. I'm Tessa. I'm one of the social

workers here at the hospital. I was wondering if I might speak to you for a few minutes?" She smiled politely at Anna, waiting for her to leave.

"Yeah, sure." Kylie opened the bedside table, removing her purse. She pulled a five-dollar bill out and handed it to Anna.

"Hey, would you mind grabbing me a candy bar from the vending machine? The food here is crap. Get yourself something too."

Anna nodded as she took the money and left the room.

By the time Anna returned to the room, Kylie was all smiles. She sat on the bed, clasping her purse.

"I can go home."

"So soon?"

"The social worker lady made me agree to go see a therapist. She was kind enough to make me an appointment at their clinic. Ten tomorrow morning. Woo hoo," she added snarkily.

Anna handed her a candy bar. "Well, um. Okay then, I guess we should go. Do you have to sign some papers or something?"

"Yeah, the nurse is going to bring them in a minute. Truth be told, I'm kinda done with this whole hospital scene, ya know? I'm gonna go wait at the nurses' station." Unwrapping the candy bar, she took a large bite as she walked out the door."

Anna glanced around the sad space, turning to follow Kylie's lead.

****

"Why did you do it?" Anna whispered. "Were you trying to kill yourself again?"

"No." Kylie stared out the car window. Anna was

still surprised the hospital didn't admit Kylie. She picked her up from the hospital within a few hours of Kylie getting there. They were on their way back home.

"You wouldn't understand. I'll move out as soon as I find another place. Then I won't be in your way." Kylie continued to stare at her lap as she zipped and unzipped her oversized purse. The sound of the zipper was beginning to grate on Anna's nerves. She could feel her shoulders inching closer toward her ears. She took a slow, deep breath and tried to relax her muscles.

"Believe it or not, you're not in my way. I care about you. I want to understand. What's going on? Why did you cut yourself so much?"

Kylie remained silent.

"Kylie, I can't ignore this stuff. If you are going to live in my house, I need to know what's going on."

"To feel something," Kylie whispered.

"What?"

"Haven't you ever hurt so much inside, you just had to do something to your outside?"

"No," Anna lied. She stared at Kylie in silence.

Kylie continued, "To prove to myself I was still alive. To let some of the poison out. It's like…"

"To prove you are alive?" Anna spit out the words. "You could have killed yourself!"

"Oh please, they weren't deep. Trust me; I've done worse."

I'm out of my league. But I can't suddenly kick her out. Can I? What the heck did I get myself into?

As they pulled up in front of the house, Anna turned the car off and grabbed Kylie's hand.

"Look, I don't know what you've been through. But I want to help you. Please, please promise me you won't do that again." Kylie moved her hand out from under Anna's.

"If I promised that, I would be lying." Kylie opened the car door and stepped outside.

Anna followed her into the house, closing the door behind them. Kylie moved toward the couch and sat down, tucking her feet underneath her.

"Why don't you just kick me out?" she asked.

"Because I care about what happens to you. I want to make sure you're okay."

"It makes no sense," Kylie said, laying her head down on the arm of the velvety couch. "Why would you *care* about me? You barely know me."

Anna came over to the couch and sat down on the cushion beside her.

"I care because you are in my life now. I care because you're important. I don't know how to explain it. But I believe everything happens for a reason. Sometimes people come into our lives to teach us something, even if we don't understand it. I feel this connection to you, and I suspect it's been a long time since you've let anyone get close."

"I tried." Kylie snorted and wiped at her nose. "Look where it got me. It sounds to me like you're trying to work off some kind of Catholic guilt or some shit like that."

Anna slid closer to her, curiosity outweighing the rule she put in place of trying to respect Kylie's privacy by not getting too involved.

"Kylie, what happened to you?"

Kylie paused, reaching for the decorative throw pillow next to her. She studied its floral design, fingering the blue tassels attached. Exhaling, she began speaking in a monotone voice. Her face seemed void of emotion. A heaviness filled the air.

"I guess after you are raped once, being raped again shouldn't be a big deal. Right?"

Before Anna could respond, Kylie continued.

"I was raped when I was sixteen. Because the guy who did it was my uncle, my dad didn't believe me. He kicked me out of the house and said I'd seduced his brother. I guess my mom didn't know what to do, so she didn't do much of anything. My friend Tasha was a lot older than me. She'd already graduated from high school, gotten a job, and had her own apartment. She let me move in with her. I thought I was home free, but pretty soon, I found out what her job entailed. Nothing is for *free*, ya know?

"For a while, she let me partner with her. We had quite a business going until I started sampling too many drugs. Then, I got hooked. For a while, I was on the streets. It was bad. I was so out of it I didn't even know who I was anymore. I'd be walking the streets, trying to make money however I could. One day I went into a church for a free meal. This woman, Susan, ended up somehow talking me into going into rehab. She'd been an addict herself and cleaned up her act. She was a miracle worker. She helped me get off the street, and I've been clean ever since."

How horrible! What do I say? Anna's eyes were full of tears. *No wonder Kylie has nightmares.*

"I am so sorry." Anna didn't know how else to respond.

Kylie ignored her and kept playing with the tassels on the pillow. One of them looked as though it would fall off due to the severe rubbing. Before Anna could even try to say something comforting, Kylie continued.

"So, you would think that after all these years, when it happened again, it wouldn't be such a big deal, right?" Her eyes welled up with tears and spilled down her cheeks.

Anna moved closer to her on the couch and reached for her hand. Surprisingly, Kylie let her.

"The night you found me on the bridge…that night was so much worse." She paused and took a deep breath.

"Kylie, you don't have to tell—"

"No, you should know. You should know what you're up against. The night on the bridge, I was ready. Ready to jump. I mean, *what the fuck;* who gets raped *twice?* Do I send out some sort of vibe? Was I asking for it?" She paused a moment and took a deep breath. Anna's mind whirled as she tried to think of something to say.

"I'd gotten out of work late and was starving. I could smell the pizza and beer before I even got to the door. I remember being irked that my housemates had friends over because I really wanted a peaceful night so I could go to sleep. The music was blaring. As soon as I got in the door, I could tell they were all drunk. I mean, w*ay* drunk. I went into the kitchen, poured myself a diet soda, and grabbed a slice. One of them must have put something in my drink, cuz after a few minutes, I started feeling super dizzy and confused. The next thing I remember, I was on the couch, and they were taking turns with me."

Kylie sobbed and started shaking.

"Oh Kylie, I'm so…" Anna's stomach clenched as she tried to think of the right words to say.

"There were three of them." She paused to grab a tissue and smeared it under each eye.

"Later, when I woke up, they were gone. Get this; there was a note saying *Thanks for the party last night!* What nerve! I knew I had to get out of there and never go back. After I walked around downtown for a bit, I realized there was nothing left to live for. No one would even miss me." Kylie started to sob again. Her body was shaking, and the tears were flowing so hard they were dripping down the front of her shirt.

Anna reached up and gently wiped them away.

"I would have missed you."

Anna put her arm around Kylie, and they cried together.

Chapter 6

Anna

Anna slid out from under Kylie's arm. The couch cushions were smushed with the weight of both women. A small throw pillow lay precariously on the edge of the armrest. After the confession, she hadn't been quite sure how to respond. The women sat in silence for several minutes. Anna kept her arm around Kylie's shoulder. Her mind whirled, and she wished she could somehow piece together the perfect words to comfort Kylie—a verbal analgesic to soothe the soul.

After several more minutes of silence, it became apparent by Kylie's soft snoring she was asleep. The remote was too far away to reach without getting up. Anna's arm was heavy with pins and needles from the awkward position into which it was cramped. She stood up and stretched her neck until she felt the familiar crack she needed. Grabbing the knit throw from the back of the armchair, she gingerly placed it over Kylie. Once in the kitchen, she sighed and filled the kettle with fresh water. Turning on the burner, she grabbed her favorite mug and stood staring out the window above the sink. Dusk was already approaching. Its dim solitude wrapping her in a comforting hug. She stood transfixed and lost in thought until the whistle of the kettle startled her back to the reality of her little kitchen.

What am I supposed to do? Why do I even care so much? I'm in over my head. She needs help. More help than I can give her.

Anna made herself a cup of steaming tea and took it back into the living room. Kylie was still asleep. Her feet were now up on the couch, and the blanket was pulled up higher. Anna picked up the remote and sat near Kylie's feet. She spread the remainder of the afghan over her lap and flicked on the TV. Flipping channels with the TV muted, Anna couldn't calm her racing mind. She turned and studied Kylie. Her long black hair was askew with random tangles. Her closed lids graced remnants of an icy pink shadow. Her mascara smeared so much; a faint smudge stuck to the hollows under each eye. A smattering of tiny freckles ran across the bridge of her nose, and a small mole dotted the skin under the corner of her left eye. Anna moved closer, feeling Kylie's breath expel in small puffs. She could smell cigarettes and vanilla. Kylie's lips were slightly parted in slumber, and she noticed how soft they looked. A strange feeling crept down her spine, reminding her of the time Bobby Dillar kissed her back in fourth grade. Suddenly Kylie stirred, opened her eyes, and sat up.

"What the hell are you doing?"

"N-nothing. I was watching TV. I was trying to be quiet and let you sleep," Anna replied, inching her way back toward the other end of the sofa.

"Were you gonna…kiss me?"

"What? No!"

Kylie grinned, licking her lips and easing her way toward Anna.

"No, I mean, I'm not into *women*," Anna stammered.

"You're kidding, right?" Kylie chortled. "You totally are. Do you have a boyfriend?"

"Well, no. But that doesn't mean—"

"Anna, be serious with me. It's the twenty-first century! Are you embarrassed?"

Anna squeezed the pillow she managed to grab and hold on her lap. She sat in stunned silence, unsure of how to respond. Her mind raced with questions, but she recognized the familiar flutter settling in her stomach.

"When was the last time you had a date?" Kylie's tone was not unkind. It was simply blunt.

"What? I mean, it was a while ago. Why?" She paused. "You've got it all wrong. I don't even know what to say to you right now."

Kylie continued to stare at her with a smirk on her face.

"Okay, whatever. You've got the wrong idea. I, I was not gonna kiss you. I am not a lesbian. I…was just sitting here, being quiet so you could sleep," Anna whispered. They sat in silence for a long moment. As Kylie began inching closer, Anna remained frozen in place. Her brain told her to move, to speak up, to *do something*! But her breath caught in her throat, and she felt the pull toward Kylie as their lips touched. *She's so soft.*

Kylie placed her hand in Anna's hair, and Anna closed her eyes, lost in the moment. She responded with a soft moan.

Then, right before their lips touched again, Kylie pulled away remaining silent until she stood up and sauntered away.

****

Anna was exhausted from Kylie's emotional disclosure yesterday. She felt drained and her head was throbbing. Her shoulders were so tight it felt as if she was carrying cement around. She was in no mood for therapy today. In addition to discovering she left her wallet at home when she attempted to pay for her groceries, she lost one of her favorite earrings and double-booked two of her customers. By the time she was in for the night last night and ready for a relaxing evening of TV show binge-watching, her head was pounding. Since her stupid HMO only allowed for eight migraine pills per month, she always tried to stretch the pills out as long as possible. Despite her best efforts, she was usually out of pills by the middle of the month. Often, caffeine, aspirin, and ibuprofen were used throughout the week until the pain became unbearable, and she had to give in and take the pill. It was ridiculous because if she just took the pill at the beginning stages of the migraine, it usually helped. Every month she ran out of pills, she prayed her concoction would keep her from heading to urgent care or the emergency room with the pain. What was the point of going there anyway? The fluorescent lights alone would drive her mad.

Last night's migraine had morphed into a morning of even more pain. Luckily, she only had two haircuts scheduled in the morning and wasn't planning on returning to work after her therapy appointment. She managed to get through the cuts while maintaining a loose professional courtesy, and by the time she arrived at Sheila's office, she was exhausted and in survival mode.

While sitting in the waiting room, she opened a silver blister packet, popping the last remaining pill onto her tongue and letting it dissolve. It filled her mouth with an acidic false-peppermint taste.

When Sheila opened her office door to let her in, Anna was opening an overly caffeinated can of soda.

The satisfying fizzy pop filled the air.

"Tough day?" Sheila asked.

Anna set the drink down on a rainbow coaster and settled onto the couch. "You could say that."

"What's going on? You look like you don't feel so great."

"I've been dealing with a migraine since last night."

"I'm sorry." Sheila paused, a silence filling the air while she waited for Anna to continue.

"I think I made a mistake inviting Kylie to live with me. I don't know what I was thinking."

"Tell me more about that," Sheila invited.

Picking at her cuticle, Anna sighed. "Well, it turns out she is pretty messed up. I mean, I know everyone has problems, but I'm not sure I can help her with hers."

"Why do you think you need to be the one to help her?"

Anna knew this was a good point. She still had a bit of a savior complex. It often started with her latching on to someone who needed her, her trying very hard to help that person, and eventually facing the realization there was very little she could ultimately do to help them. She took a swig of her citrus soda before continuing.

"Isn't helping others a good thing?" she countered.

"I mean, isn't helping what we are here to do?"

Sheila waited for her to continue.

Sometimes therapy frustrated Anna. It felt like Sheila already knew the answers to the questions she was asking her. She just wanted to hear Anna say it out loud. She'd been meeting with Sheila on and off for the past few years. Despite her level of comfort here, she still found herself filtering her responses before sharing them. A part of her always wanted to be a model patient by learning from her mistakes and answering questions with great insight. Yet, she kept repeating the same stupid mistakes over and over.

"What are you thinking about?" Sheila asked.

"Henry." As soon as she said his name, she regretted bringing it up.

"Hmm." Sheila nodded as she pushed at the bridge of her oversized glasses. "What about Henry?"

"I wasn't able to help him," she continued after watching Sheila raise her eyebrows. "I mean, I did help him, a bit...but then he left anyway."

"Ahh. Do you think you are more concerned with helping Kylie or with the fact she might leave too?"

Anna stared out the window. She didn't like the question.

"How do you feel about her being a stripper?" Anna's therapist asked.

"I'm not sure. I mean, it could have been worse. She isn't a prostitute. She dances for money. A lot of money. I think she was afraid I would kick her out or something because she tried to pay for a full year's worth of rent. I compromised by letting her pay for six months. I didn't realize how much would change in six months."

"Like what?"

"I'm not sure where to start," Anna replied. Tears sprang to her eyes. She tried to swipe them away.

"Why don't you start with what's making you cry?" Sheila suggested.

"I don't even know why I'm crying." Anna started to laugh uncomfortably as the tears continued to flow. "It's been happening a lot lately."

"Crying?"

"Yeah, except I'm not sure why I'm crying. Like, I'll be scrubbing out the sink, and then out of the blue, I'll start crying."

"Let's go back to that for a moment. Can you remember what you were thinking about while you were scrubbing the sink?"

Anna picked at her nail polish. "I wasn't thinking about anything in particular. I was simply scrubbing the sink. I might have been thinking, 'The sink is gross, I need to clean it.' "

"Hmm. Okay, let's pause at you thinking about the sink being dirty. What happened right before you started scrubbing it?"

Anna was getting annoyed. What was the point of this? She would try to humor Sheila.

"Um, I finished washing the dishes." The statement came out sounding ruder than she intended. She gave Sheila a small smile.

Sheila smiled back and continued. "I'm wondering what you were thinking about while you were washing the dishes."

Silence filled the room. Anna wished Sheila would drop it. If she was hunting for some big breakthrough, Anna was going to disappoint her with the boring details of her life. The silence continued. Thinking back, she pictured herself standing at the sink. In her mind's eye, she turned off the faucet, studying the stained porcelain. Grandma's sink was always so white and clean. She would have never let her sink get so dirty. The pinprick of tears threatened the back of her eyes. She blinked and took a deep breath, willing them away. She broke the silence.

"I guess I must have been thinking about my grandmother."

"What about your grandmother?" Sheila urged. "Can you remember what might have come into your mind that made you think about her?"

"My sink?" A small chuckle. "I remembered how she taught me to keep the kitchen sink clean. It's silly, I guess. I mean, I don't know why a sink would have made me start crying."

"Is this the grandmother you lived with for a while?"

Anna nodded.

"And, how long ago did she pass away?"

"Close to ten years ago."

"Sometimes those small memories we carry around with us are a reminder of how much we cared for another person. Can you remember how you were feeling when you were thinking of your grandmother and her sink?"

"Sad."

"You felt sad. She was a big part of your life."

"Yes," agreed Anna, "she was. I still miss her."

****

For the next few days, Anna tried her best to stay out of Kylie's way. It wasn't until Kylie cornered her in the bathroom, forcing her to confront the incident consuming her thoughts of late.

She'd been blow-drying her hair when Kylie opened the door and approached her from behind. She was so surprised by the tap on her shoulder; she dropped the dryer onto the floor. It continued to whir for a moment until she reached down, grabbed it, and turned it off.

"We need to talk," Kylie said.

"I'm kind of busy. I have to finish getting ready for work."

"You can't fucking avoid me forever. If you want to keep giving me the silent treatment, I can handle it. I'm an expert at it.

"I'm not giving you the silent treatment."

"It sure feels like it."

"I don't know what you want me to say to you right—" Anna's thought was interrupted by a sneeze. "—now."

"Well, how many more years are you gonna ignore it?" Kylie asked, while handing Anna a tissue.

"Ignore what? Geez, Kylie, you've got a lot of nerve. You waltz in here and pretend you know everything about me? We barely know each other—" Anna sneezed again and grabbed the box of tissues from the counter.

"No shit, Sherlock. You let me stay here, a complete stranger. You see how fucked up my life is, and I know nothing about you. You're locked up as tight as a rusted sunken treasure."

Anna sneezed again. Then she sneezed three more times in a row. She held a tissue over her mouth and nose in hopes of holding the rest in.

"Look," Anna began. Then she sneezed so forcefully she whacked her head on the countertop as her body bent with the impact. She stood and stumbled to sit on the toilet lid, her palm pressed against her forehead. "Oh. That hurts. Am I bleeding?"

Kylie bent to pull her hand away.

"No. It's red, but it's not bleeding. Holy…you *are* already getting a goose egg." Kylie stepped back to regard her. "You look like shit."

Anna stood and peered into the mirror. She started to laugh, a slight chuckle at first, but soon found her laugh growing into a heaving guffaw. She held her stomach as she continued to laugh louder and harder.

Kylie studied her, and despite her best efforts, couldn't resist joining in. Soon both women were belly laughing.

"I'm a mess." Anna sneezed and started to laugh again. "Owww! My head is killing me." A whimper escaped mid-laugh. Then she started to cry.

Kylie sat on the side of the tub. She remained silent while Anna switched back and forth from crying to sneezing to laughing. When she had composed herself, she locked eyes with Kylie.

"You must think I'm mental."

"*You're* mental? Ha! Which one of us was on the ledge of a bridge?" Kylie chortled.

Silence filled the stuffy room for a second, and both women burst into laughter again.

Chapter 7

Anna

The rest of the week was uneventful. Anna saw a handful of regular clients and even had a few new walk-ins at the salon. Kylie was quiet and calm, and for once, almost seemed happy. Anna wondered if she'd imagined some of the drama from the earlier weeks and often allowed her mind to wander to the evening when Kylie fell asleep beside her on the couch. On Friday afternoon, Helen came into Snip and Shape for her regular wash and set.

"Ahhh, sweetie, you're in love, aren't ya?" Helen coughed and tried to cover a smile.

"What? What are you talking about?" Anna turned off the faucet and wrapped Helen's silvery hair in a warm, fluffy towel. As Anna started to help her stand and walk back toward her station, Helen stopped, then lightly touched Anna's arm. Her hands were as soft as velvet on Anna's bare skin.

"I see the telltale signs, my dear," she rasped. "You keep staring off into space with a goofy expression on your face, and you can't stop smiling." Helen started coughing again.

"Helen, you need to stop smoking." Anna tried to change the subject.

"Honey, I could keel over and die any second. Do

you really think I'm going to stop now? I've cut down, seems good enough to me. And, I don't have Alzheimer's yet, so stop trying to distract me. So, who is the lucky fellow?"

Anna paused, guiding Helen to the swivel chair and grabbing a comb.

"I am *not* in love," she said as she started to comb out the wiry knots.

Helen nodded thoughtfully but remained silent.

****

Anna pulled up to the driveway and saw a beat-up red pickup in her driveway. As she unlocked the front door, she jumped back. Kylie stood in the entranceway.

"Geez! You scared me!"

Kylie ignored the scolding, pulling Anna inside and squeezing her tight.

"Did you see my new truck? Isn't she great? My dad used to have a truck like this," she rambled. "I can't believe what a good deal I got on it! Now I don't have to take the bus to work anymore. I'm so excited!"

"I can tell, geez. Slow down, Kylie. Where did you get it?"

"I know a guy." Kylie snort-laughed, pulling Anna into the living room and onto the couch.

"So, how was your day?" Kylie asked as she scooted up closer to Anna.

"It was fine, nothing special. I guess I'm a bit tired from being on my feet all day."

Kylie scooped up Anna's ankles and placed her feet on her lap. She flipped off Anna's shoes and began rubbing the arch of the closest foot.

"Kylie, you don't have—"

"Shhh, it's fine. You worry too much. Relax.

Doesn't it feel good?"

Anna hesitated for a second, then sank back into the cushions and closed her eyes.

"My mom used to do this to me when I was a little girl," Anna whispered.

"What were your parents like? Where are they now? I mean, are they still around?"

"They were great. I mean, I was an only child, so I guess they sort of spoiled me. Not that I minded. My mom was so artistic. She painted these beautiful landscapes. My dad insisted on hanging them all over the house. My dad, he used to read to me all the time. He would take me out to concerts and coffeehouses, and museums. The three of us were always going somewhere." Her eyes clouded over and filled with tears.

"What happened to them?"

"My mom died when I was in high school. My dad started drinking again. I mean, he got sober when I was little, but it didn't last. He's still around, in a way. I mean, he has what's called frontal lobe dementia. He doesn't remember who I am anymore." Her voice was so quiet Kylie moved closer in order to hear her.

"I'm so sorry."

Anna started to pull her feet away, but Kylie grabbed them and held them in her lap.

"It was a car accident. They were on their way to visit me at college, and someone…it was a hit-and-run. They never found the driver of the other car. Anyway, my life changed forever. I was eighteen. It was my freshman year. So, I dropped out, helped my dad take care of the details, and I never went back. My dad started losing his memory a few years ago. He lives with my aunt in Buffalo now."

"I didn't know you went to college," said Kylie.

"Well, I never went back. After the funeral, there wasn't a lot of money left. I dropped out, but I did manage to go to cosmetology school."

"I'm so sorry about your parents. It sounds like they were great people. It sucks you've lost both of them."

Anna cleared her throat and moved her legs off Kylie's lap. She did not want to cry today. Her head was already throbbing, and crying would only make it worse. She stood, smoothing her shirt. If she didn't change the subject, she was bound to cry.

"I have to run some errands."

"Now? I thought maybe we could hang out and watch a movie or something." Kylie patted the sofa, waiting for Anna to sit back down.

"Sorry. I have to get some ingredients for dinner tonight."

"We could order in," Kylie retorted.

Anna smiled. "Not tonight, but I'll be back soon." She walked away, leaving Kylie alone on the couch.

****

"How have things been with Kylie over the past few weeks?" Sheila asked.

Anna didn't want to admit to the feelings she was developing for Kylie. Maybe if she didn't say them out loud, they wouldn't be quite real. A part of her felt embarrassed. Here in this safe space, she still felt as though she needed to please Sheila somehow. It was as if Sheila somehow took on the role of her mother. Anna felt confused by the feelings. Had she always liked women and just didn't fully realize it, or was this specific to Kylie?

"I guess I kinda see the whole thing as a sort of sign."

"A sign? What do you mean?"

"Well, like everything happens for a reason."

"Ah yes, you've mentioned that before. It sounds like you feel Kylie is in your life for a specific reason. What do you think the reason might be?" Sheila asked.

Anna shrugged. "I'm not sure yet. I think she needs some kindness in her life. She's had it rough." Anna wrinkled her nose at Sheila's seemingly indifferent demeanor. "What?" she asked Sheila. "Do you think I made a mistake in allowing her to move in with me?"

Sheila remained silent for a few seconds. "I wouldn't necessarily say 'mistake.' I guess I'm wondering if you feel like you need to take care of her?"

"Well, yeah. I guess so."

"Anna—" Shelia paused. "—who is going to take care of you?"

****

A few days later, Anna woke to the sound of banging. At first, she thought someone was knocking at the door. As she stumbled down the hallway and into the kitchen, she squinted into the harsh morning light.

"What are you doing?"

"Did you move my keys?" Kylie's voice grew louder as she continued to open kitchen cupboards and slam them shut again.

"What? No. I didn't touch your keys. Where did you see them last?"

"If I knew that, Sherlock, I wouldn't be fucking looking for them!"

Anna flinched and took a deep breath.

"Let me help you."

"You hid them. You hid them so I couldn't go to work. You want me to get a more respectable job."

"What are you talking about?"

Without warning, Kylie grabbed a glass off the counter and threw it toward Anna. It shattered near her feet. She watched as a large shard landed near her pinky toe.

"Kylie! What is wrong with you?" Anna jumped back, heading toward the phone.

"I need my keys, Anna. I'm not kiddin'. I need to go to the mountain and make my delivery!"

"What delivery? A mountain? Kylie, what are you talking about? Calm down. I will help you find your keys."

Anna held her breath as she moved toward her, her phone tight in her sweaty palm. Before she could say anything else, Kylie pushed her way past Anna and ran down the hall. Stunned, Anna paused for a moment and turned to follow her. The bathroom door slammed shut, and she was left alone. She could hear Kylie opening and closing drawers. Anna dialed 911 with shaky fingers and tried to compose herself enough to talk without her voice rattling like an old teeter-totter.

"This is 911. What is your emergency?"

"Uh, I think my roommate is having some sort of nervous breakdown. She has hurt herself before, and now she's locked herself in the bathroom, and I…"

"What is your location, ma'am?"

"Oh, 104 Evergreen Drive."

"All right, we have an officer on the way. Please stay on the line with me. Do you feel you are in any danger?"

"Me?" Anna breathed out and slid her body down the wall, sinking into the plush carpet. She studied a brown stain near the baseboard.

"No, not me," she said. "At least not right now."

****

Two police cars pulled up in front of her house, followed by an ambulance. The lights flashed, but no sirens. She opened the door and described Kylie's bizarre behavior to the female officer. Officer Stacy Fitzpatrick made an immediate impression on her, causing Anna to smile as the policewoman tried to tame the wild red curls springing out from under her cap. Despite the messy ponytail and random tucking, the hair had a mind of its own. "Fitz," as she insisted Anna call her, had a personality to match the hair. Anna led her to the kitchen table while the other professionals talked to Kylie from outside the bathroom door and worked on picking the lock.

"Okay, so—" Fitz chewed on her pencil and pulled out a small pad of tattered paper. "—start at the beginning. Tell me what happened tonight to set your girlfriend off. Did you have a fight? Is she on anything? Does she have a history of mental illness?"

Anna wanted to start off by telling her Kylie was not her girlfriend, but honestly, she didn't even know how to categorize her anymore. She also didn't know where to start. Before she could answer any more questions, the door to the bathroom was forced open. She could hear Kylie before she could see her.

"Get off of me! Leave me alone! They're calling, just let me go…" Kylie was holding a metal nail file and started to stab herself in the arm.

Anna tried to make her way down the hall, but a second officer intercepted her.

"I'm sorry, ma'am, but you are going to have to move back and let us take care of this."

Anna felt a tug on her sleeve and turned to see Officer Fitz motioning for her to return to the kitchen. She felt as if she was caught in a slow-moving nightmare. It took two EMT workers and the other officer to hold on to Kylie and strap her down on the gurney. As they pushed it past the kitchen and toward the door, Kylie continued to thrash and scream. Her eyes reminded Anna of the feral cat she once tried to catch behind her childhood home. She succeeded in grabbing it, but while she was proudly carrying it to the house to show her parents, it bit her.

Chapter 8

Anna

A week went by before Anna was able to see Kylie in the hospital. She called every day, only to be told they could not release any information. Then, on Friday morning, the phone rang.

"Hello, may I speak to Miss Johnson?" The voice on the other end of the phone was syrupy sweet.

"Yes, this *is*."

"Miss Johnson, Debbie LaPrade. I'm a social worker at Health United Hospital. Kylie Teeter has asked me to contact you. She has signed a release form permitting us to talk with you about her condition. Would you be available to come in and meet with us?"

"Her condition? Um, yes, of course. When do you need me to come?" Anna dumped her coffee in the sink and began straightening the kitchen.

"How about one o'clock today?"

"I'll be there." Anna wrote down the details of where to go and hung up the phone. Her heart thumped, and a heaviness filled her chest. She stood and stared out the kitchen window into her small backyard.

What am I supposed to do? Should I just wash my hands of this whole thing, or am I in this situation for a reason? I feel this connection to Kylie, even an attraction—which scares me. Is this wrong? Even though she is a mess, I finally feel like something in my life has clicked into place. Something I haven't wanted to admit.

Anna turned on the faucet and washed her hands. Her cuticles were raw and ragged from picking at them all week. She sighed and patted her hands dry. Grabbing her favorite hand lotion from her purse, she applied a liberal amount and took her time rubbing it in. Cupping her hands to her nose, she inhaled the jasmine fragrance and took a deep breath. Then she turned off her mind, grabbed her keys, and headed out the door.

****

The drive to the hospital was becoming absurdly familiar. This time, she pulled into Lot J, right after the main entrance. The doors swished open, inviting her inside the cool interior of the lobby. She paused and stepped back as they closed. Anna stood frozen on the sidewalk. Transfixed by the glossy glass of the entranceway, she hesitated, as if she was a child facing the funhouse that she waited so long to visit but lost her courage.

I could leave now. Turn around and climb back in the car. It would be easier. Way easier.

She turned and headed back toward the car. She absentmindedly rubbed her stomach as it swirled with anxiety. Circling back, she forced herself through the doors before they whispered shut.

"Hi, I'm here for a meeting with Debbie LaPrade?" Anna's voice came out a pitch higher than was comfortable. She stood by the information desk as the woman behind it studied her computer screen.

"Ah yes, her one o'clock," she said. After each over-pronounced word, she snapped her candy-pink gum. "Please (*snap*) sit down (*snap, chomp-chomp*). I'll call her."

Anna conidered her options. A glum teenager and a sorrowful woman occupied two cracked and stained paisley-cushioned chairs. The bench contained a foreign family, squeezed together, speaking a dialect she didn't recognize. A plastic orange chair remained vacant. Anna was about to move in the direction of it when a tall, thin, and kind woman greeted her. The woman was young, perhaps close to Anna's age—*early thirties?*—and well dressed. She wore a gray-and-white striped A-line skirt and a white button-down silk shirt. Her simple black shoes had a small heel, and her dark brown hair was wrapped in a low bun. Her eyes reminded Anna of coffee after adding a healthy dose of creamer. A few small lines surrounded her eyes and her heartfelt smile.

"Miss Johnson?" I'm Debbie LaPrade. It's nice to meet you. Kylie has told me so much about you. Please, won't you come into my office?"

Anna attempted to walk behind the social worker to the office, but somehow the woman kept slowing her pace to walk alongside her. The office reminded Anna of a summer day. It was small but cheerful. The walls were light lilac, and a painted border of white lilies graced the top of each wall. Next to a desk piled with papers, books, and a laptop, stood a small table. The table hosted an intricate lace cloth, a small vase of fake lilies, and a box of tissues.

"Please, have a seat."

"Thank you."

"So, let's talk for a few minutes before I go get Kylie and bring her in."

"Okay." Anna sat down and moved her chair further back from the table.

"As you know, Kylie has been through a lot. Her moods aren't always stable. She has asked me to explain a little bit more to you about her diagnosis."

"Her diagnosis? What diagnosis?"

"Kylie has been diagnosed with bipolar disorder. Specifically, with bipolar I. Are you familiar with mood disorders?"

"Um, no, not so much." Anna's head was spinning with questions. *Was this why Kylie was acting so strange?*

"Bipolar is a mood disorder that affects how Kylie has been behaving lately. While here at the hospital, she began seeing Dr. Renssler, a psychiatrist. They have agreed a combination of talk therapy and daily medications may help her become more successful in dealing with this condition. Right now, Kylie is still getting used to the medications. She is no longer in a manic state but is spending much of her time sleeping—"

"Excuse me," Anna interrupted. "What do you mean by *a manic state*? Are you talking about what happened with the police and her looking for her keys? She wasn't making any sense."

"Yes. That is a good example of her mania, with a bit of psychosis. Also, it sounds like Kylie often has some mood swings and some periods of depression. Bipolar used to be called manic depression. She also appears to be struggling with paranoia and some psychosis. We would like to keep her here for a few more days under observation but wanted to talk to you and Kylie together about a safe discharge plan for her to return to the community. She will then need to continue to attend therapy once a week and will need someone to make sure she is taking her medications daily."

Anna looked up at the social worker as her eyes welled up with tears. The woman's kind face now blurred. She grabbed a tissue and wiped the tears away as fast as she could. *Why am I crying? This is not about me. It's about Kylie. She needs help.*

"Anna, I know this must be a lot to take in right now. I'm sorry. I imagine it's hard to see someone you love in so much pain. Kylie wanted me to tell you if you don't want her to come back, she understands. We can help her find housing. This is a lot for you to take on."

Anna's chair scraped against the floor as she abruptly stood. She felt confused and a bit angry.

"Kylie wanted you to tell me…where is Kylie, anyway? Why doesn't she tell me all of this herself? Why can't I see her?"

"You can see her. I can go get her right now. But, before I do, why don't we talk some more? Do you have any questions? Can I help…?"

"No. I'm tired of talking. I just want to see her."

"Of course. I'll be right back." The social worker held Anna's gaze for a second, then turned and left the room.

Anna walked over to the little window and peered outside. It was propped open with an old textbook yellowed with age and crinkled from past rainfalls. The sky was a bright blue, full of huge white fluffy clouds. A slight breeze drifted in and washed over her face. She breathed it all in and braced herself for Kylie's entrance.

****

Anna thought that her anxiety would have decreased now that Kylie was out of the house. Somehow she felt worse. The loop of repetitive thoughts that often filled her dopamine-deficient brain seemed louder and stronger. On top of that, her body was betraying her. She felt like an octogenarian. From the moment she opened her eyes in the morning, she gaged her level of pain. Would sitting up too fast make her head hurt right away? If she took some ibuprofen with her first cup of coffee, would it keep the headache from turning into a migraine? Her mind quickly scrolled through the day, imagining all of the scenarios that could play out. Somehow, she managed to drag herself from bed. The steaming hot shower that often helped her relax did nothing to alleviate her pain. Finally, after popping two ibuprofen, an aspirin, and a huge magnesium supplement, she relented and called off from work. After hanging up, she called Sheila and scheduled a last-minute appointment.

"Would you like some water?" The therapist poured an icy glass from the crystal on the table in front of her. Anna couldn't stop hiccupping.

"Are you okay?"

"No. I mean, I haven't done this hiccupping thing in a very long time. It used to happen all the time when I was a kid, and I got upset. One time it lasted for almost three hours."

"Wow. Sounds stressful. Can you tell me what's going on?" she asked as she handed Anna the glass.

"Henry came back." Anna hiccupped so loudly that she covered her mouth with one hand.

"You mean your former roommate? The one who

left after he got sick?"

Anna could feel the blush creeping into her cheeks. Another hiccup escaped.

"I haven't told you the entire story," she admitted.

Sheila gave her a small smile but remained silent.

The clock's ticking on the wall grew louder as Anna braced herself to spill the truth weighing on her mind and body.

"Henry was the father of my baby."

Chapter 9

Anna

Kylie had been home now for five days and was still spending the majority of time in her room. Occasionally, Anna would peek in and bring her a plate of food, and each time Kylie would send her away.

"Come on, Kylie, you've got to eat." Anna half-heartedly knocked on the bedroom door for the second time that day. She opened the door with one hand while holding an iced coffee in the other. She was surprised to see Kylie out of bed and stripping the sheets off the bed. The curtains were opened, and the previously littered floor was now clean.

"Hey." Kylie smiled and motioned for Anna to enter.

"Oh, you're feeling better?"

"Yeah, a bit. Thanks for letting me come back. You didn't have to."

"It's no problem." Anna picked at a cuticle and sighed. "That's what friends are for, right?"

Kylie reached for Anna's hand. "Is that what we are, *friends*?"

Anna paused. "Yes." She positioned herself in the doorway, wiping away beads of condensation from the plastic cup still in her hand. "We are good friends, Kylie. Just *friends*. I care about you, and you are welcome to stay here. But right now, I've gotta head to work. Maybe we can talk more later?" She turned to leave, then paused and faced Kylie again. "I almost forgot, here, I got this for you." She smiled and handed her the coffee. Wiping her hand on her jeans, she walked away.

****

During her lunch break, Anna flipped open her phone. *Two missed calls.* She swiped her fingers across the screen of her phone to reveal the same number listed as calling her earlier in the day. She recognized the number, and her hand slightly shook as she prepared to listen to her voicemail.

"Hey Annie, it's Henry. I'm in town for the week. I know it's been a while…Uh, can we meet up for coffee or something? Call me back this time. Come on, Annie, look, it's water under the bridge or dam or whatever, right? Call me. I'm sorry. I want to see you. I miss you."

Anna slammed her phone shut and marched back to her station. She stared at her reflection and sighed, trying to push away the flood of emotions threatening to ruin her day. How could she even carry a glimmer of kindness toward him after he hurt her so deeply? *Henry, why couldn't you just stay away?*

Concentrating on work for the remainder of the day proved to be more difficult than she bargained for. She tried her best to be cheerful and kind to each of her customers but often found herself lost in thought while playing back the last three years of her life in her mind. To her delight, her last client of the day canceled, so she could go home early. When she pulled up to the house, she felt a bit relieved to see Kylie wasn't there yet. Taking it as a sign, she let herself in the front door, kicked off her shoes, and pulled out her phone. She put the kettle on for tea and dialed Henry's number before she lost her nerve and changed her mind.

"Annie! I was beginning to think you weren't going to call back." The sound of Henry's voice on the line instantly made Anna feel nostalgic. She blinked back tears and cleared her throat.

"I didn't think I was going to call you back if I'm being completely honest." She paused.

"I'm glad you did. Will you meet me for coffee? Hear me out?" Anna could hear the discomfort in Henry's voice. She let the uncomfortable silence sting him a bit more while she took her time pouring herself a mug of tea.

"Are you still there?" he asked.

"Yes. I'm thinking." She paused again. Part of her wanted to make him squirm, while another part wanted to see him right away. "Can't you say whatever you want to say to me now, over the phone?" She knew what he would say before he replied.

"I could, but I'd much rather talk in person. I'm so sorry I hurt you. Will you please let me see you? Even just for a few minutes? I promise you can leave anytime you want, even if I want to keep talking. Please?"

The tea scalded her tongue and the roof of her mouth as she gulped the first piping hot swallow. "Okay." She coughed. "Where?"

****

Her bulky purse kept hitting her thigh as she walked into the coffee shop. It thumped in conjunction with the music. They agreed to meet at a local hot spot where they used to hang out. Henry was already seated.

Anna's heart skipped a beat as she noticed he was clean-shaven. She's always preferred him that way. His jet-black hair looked as if he'd tumbled right out of bed, but Anna knew he had likely spent several extra minutes and products to make it appear perfect. She eased her way into the booth and sighed as she saw he'd already ordered her favorite, chocolate chai latte. He smiled and handed her the cup.

"Be careful. It's hot."

"Thanks." Anna reached for the cup. She did not plan on being won over so easily. Charm and generosity only went so far. They stared at each other for a second in silence before he began talking.

"I'm sorry. Let me start by apologizing," he said.

Anna became aware of the throbbing in her forehead and around her eyes. She absentmindedly began pinching the bridge of her nose.

"I should have never left like that. It was a shitty thing for me to do to you."

"It *was* a *very* shitty thing for you to do." Anna leaned forward. "So why did you do it? Why couldn't you talk to me? You just left. After all we'd been through together. You walked away without even a backward glance." Despite her resolve to remain calm and not let her emotions get the best of her, she began crying. The pain in her forehead had grown into what she referred to as a helmet of pain, a wide band starting around her eyes and covering her entire head and neck. Besides Henry, no one in the crowded, mismatched room paid her any attention.

"I'm sorry. I know I hurt you."

"Why?" Anna repeated, wiping her eyes.

"It was all too much."

"What was? Me? I was too much?"

"No, not you. You were perfect. You *are* perfect. The sadness. *My* sadness. It was swallowing me up. I couldn't be the person you needed me to be. The person you *deserved.*"

"I didn't *deserve* for you to *leave* like that. With no warning? With no explanation? I didn't deserve to be treated *that way,* Henry. *Especially* after all we've been through."

"I know. You're right. You're beyond right. You didn't. And I'll never be able to make it up to you. But will you at least let me try?"

"What? Were you expecting to waltz right back into my life? After all this time? You show up one day, and what, expect us to pick up right where we left off?" She swallowed down the last of her chai, not caring or noticing its temperature. "You know what?" She grabbed her purse and stood. "No."

Henry watched her pull on her coat. He stood but made no move to stop her.

"No," she repeated. "You don't deserve to even ask me to accept your apology. No."

Henry watched her walk past the worn velvet couch full of teenage girls. He watched her exit the building, the tinkling chimes on the door masking the intensity of the situation.

Chapter 10

Anna

"I saw Henry," Anna announced as she plopped down on the couch beside Kylie.

"Who is Henry?"

"My ex-boyfriend," she grunted.

"Why haven't I heard about him before? How long were you together? How long ago did you break up? Geez, you sure are tight-lipped, Anna." Kylie tossed the magazine she'd been flipping through onto the coffee table, giving Anna her full attention.

After leaving the coffeehouse, Anna ended up driving around aimlessly until she felt a bit calmer. By the time she arrived back home, her headache was worse. She pulled a small bottle of over-the-counter painkiller out of her purse from beside her.

"We were together for two years before he got sick. After I helped nurse him back to health, he left me. To be honest, it's way more complicated than that. While he was in chemo, I got pregnant." She paused and smiled, taking a deep breath and exhaling. Kylie's eyes grew wider as she watched Anna.

"We were so thrilled, you know? We got engaged. Things started getting better and better with him in remission." Anna helped herself to Kylie's drink, swallowing the pills down.

"Then, I lost the baby. A few months later, he just up and left. No warning, no discussion, he just disappeared."

"Bastard!" Kylie grabbed Anna's hand. "Geez! What right does he have coming back here now? What does he want?"

"I guess he wanted to apologize. I'm not sure."

Kylie dumped a heaping spoonful of sugar into her cup. "Well, what do *you* want?"

"I thought I knew, but now I'm not so sure."

Kylie took Anna's hands between her own. "Well, I'm not going anywhere. You're my best friend. You saved me. I know I am a bit of a mess, but at least I don't leave when the going gets tough."

Anna stirred her tea some more. She stared at the clock on the wall while continuing to stir. Best friend? They haven't even known each other very long. How was it so easy for Kylie to attach herself without regard to risk? What were they doing, anyway? Was this even *friendship?* She heard Kylie's words, but they sounded as if they were coming from far away. It was as if she was stuck outside in a snowstorm and someone was shouting, but she couldn't quite make out what was being said. She watched Kylie as if in slow motion. The colors surrounding them appeared momentarily muted. What was wrong with her? She rubbed the back of her neck and squeezed her eyes shut for an extra second. Lights began flickering behind her closed lids. When she opened her eyes, the vision in her left eye was hazy.

"What's wrong? Don't you believe me?" Kylie's voice rose into a small whine.

"What? Oh, sorry. No, I mean, yes. I have a migraine. I'm going to go lie down for a few minutes."

Anna stood up. Swaying a bit, she grabbed the side of the table to correct her stance. She was about to walk to her room when Kylie surprised her with kindness yet again.

"Here, let me help you." She put her arm around Anna's waist and guided her down the hall. Once in her room, she helped her onto the bed. She covered her with the blanket. Anna's eyes were already closed. Kylie exhaled and crept out of the room.

****

"So, do you feel that you have always been attracted to women?" Anna's therapist leaned forward in her chair. Silence fell on the room like a thick wool blanket. The therapist waited. The clock ticked. The furnace clicked on. She hated when silence was used as a prompt to explore a particularly touchy subject.

"I guess." The words stuck in the base of her throat. Tears trickled down her cheeks onto her flannel shirt.

Sheila sat back. "Can you tell me why you are crying?" Her voice was full of kindness.

"I've never admitted that to anyone before. I guess it makes it feel more real."

"Hmm. Did it not feel real before?"

"I dunno. I mean, I try not to think about it."

"Why's that?"

Anna picked at a stray cuticle. She knew Sheila would notice this but no longer cared.

"Well, I don't spend a lot of time thinking about it. It was something that was always there, but I guess I never thought of it as a real option."

"I see. Why?" she pressed.

"You know why. My religion. I mean, growing up,

everything was about religion. It was my whole world." She peeled a small chunk of skin away from her thumbnail. The pressure in her forehead building as the tears pricked behind her eyes. She choked out the answers to the therapist's questions without looking at her.

"And same-sex attraction was not allowed in your religion?"

"No way!" Anna scoffed. "If my parents found out, I think they would damn me to hell! No doubt they'd start a prayer chain for me."

"A prayer chain? What is a prayer chain?"

"It's when they start calling all these people in their church and ask them to all pray for me."

"I see. Your tone seems to suggest you wouldn't want that to happen. Am I right?"

"Um, well, I mean—I guess I should take all the prayers I can get, right? I really don't know what I believe anymore."

"I imagine it must have made things even more difficult for you."

More tears spilled down Anna's cheeks.

Sheila waited. "Have you ever been physical with a woman before?"

"No, not really. I mean, I kissed a girl in junior high, but I'm not sure that counts. I didn't even date anyone in high school. My first boyfriend was in college."

"Mm-hmm." Shelia nodded, prompting her to say more.

"What?" Anna smiled. "You're wondering if I liked it, right? When I kissed the girl? It was fine. I mean, good. It was good. But I like men. I guess I like women too? Ugh. What is wrong with me?"

"Anna, I don't see anything wrong with you at all. Do you know any other bisexuals?"

Anna paused, considering her options. She hadn't really thought of herself as a bisexual, just a confused person in pain. She wasn't accustomed to acknowledging her emotional pain. She usually unconsciously shoved it aside to make room for everything else. Physical pain had been her bedfellow for so long that she often forgot to identify herself in any other way. It was often her first thought upon waking, and the last thing on her mind at the end of the day. Being bisexual was never in her vocabulary. The word alone made her bristle. Sheila used it so casually, as if it was an everyday occurrence. Anna remained silent, allowing the Herculean shift to flow through her.

Chapter 11

Kylie

"So, you're Anna's new roommate?" Henry sized Kylie up, staring at her a few seconds too long. His eyes lingered on her decorated shoulders. She noticed he tried not to look at her chest, but like all men, he couldn't stop himself.

"I'm her *best* friend." Kylie nearly cut him off. "We also happen to be roommates."

"I see," he replied sarcastically. "And did she send you here to meet me or something?"

"No. Anna doesn't even know I'm here. She'd probably be pretty mad if she found out I was."

"So, let me get this straight. You're her *best friend,* and she *doesn't* know you're here? You must not know her very well if you think that move isn't gonna piss her off." He laughed.

Kylie shrugged and squeezed her way in front of him, heading toward a table.

Pausing for a second, he glanced around as if being watched, then followed her.

They sat in uncomfortable silence until the waitress arrived. After ordering, the silence resumed. Henry excused himself to use the bathroom, and by the time he returned, their appetizers were on the table. Henry dipped a handful of fries into the ketchup and stuffed them in his mouth. Kylie sipped her milkshake and watched him over the straw. He swallowed and cleared his throat.

"So, not to be rude or anything, but what is it you want?" he asked.

"I want you to stay the hell away from Anna. That's what I want." Kylie saw the surprise in his eyes as his brows lifted slightly. "She is over you. And besides, she is spoken for."

"Oh yeah?" He leaned back in his chair, stretching his long legs. "So, who is this guy, anyway? When did he come into the picture? Do you know him?"

Kylie grinned. "You could say that." She stared at him coldly and leaned forward. "She's with me."

Henry sat up abruptly, pushing his chair back slightly. It scraped along the linoleum, causing the family at the booth beside them to turn and look. "Huh? Wait a second. Are you saying…? No. Are you saying Anna is *with* you—as in you are a *couple*?"

Kylie gave a satisfied nod.

"I don't believe it. Anna would never…No, I mean, we were together for a while, and she never gave me the impression she wasn't totally straight. I mean, she seemed perfectly happy."

"You mean until you left her?"

Silence hung between them.

"Look, I've got to talk to Anna about this. I don't believe it. I know I made a mistake, but it doesn't mean I turned her off of men completely!"

"It doesn't work that way," said Kylie. "Leave her alone. You've hurt her enough. Let her move on with her life."

Henry stood, scooping up his leftovers and

dropping them onto his tray. "Where is she? Is she home? We need to talk."

"Why? So you can try to win her back? Don't bother. She's over you."

He eyed Kylie cautiously, then sat back down.

"I didn't come here to cause trouble."

"Then what *did* you come here for?'

"I, I'm not sure." He smoothed his hair. "Not that it's any of your business."

Kylie started to interrupt, but he beat her to it.

"No offense, but I think we're done here." He pulled out a twenty-dollar bill and threw it on the table. "My treat. I'm going to find Anna." He stood, tucking his wallet into the back pocket of his faded Levis. Kylie held her tongue as she watched him saunter away. She might give him a head start to the house, but he was not going to have the final word.

****

By the time Henry pulled into Anna's driveway, Kylie had caught up. She parked by the curb and ran after him as he pounded on the door.

"Anna. Let me in. I need to talk to you." Henry's knocking got louder while Kylie watched in amusement. "Anna! Anna! Open the door!"

"You know *I* have a key, right? I do live here too." She smirked.

Henry ignored her and rang the bell. The door swung open to reveal a dripping wet Anna. A large white towel covered her body; another fluffy pink one enveloped her hair.

"Geez! What's all the racket? I was in the shower. Kylie? What is going on? Why are you just standing there? Why didn't you let him in?"

"Let *him* in?" Kylie shouted. "Why didn't you *tell* me you were seeing him again?"

Anna secured her towel and sighed. "Seeing him? Come in, Henry. Kylie, are you coming too?"

Kylie pushed her way past Henry and stormed into the house. She dashed into her room and grabbed the robe off the back of her door. Rushing back to Anna, she shoved it toward her.

"Put something on, for crying out loud!"

Henry paused in the foyer. His gaze took in the new paint and décor. He followed the women into the living room and sat down in the chair opposite the couch where they were settling. The thick weight of unspoken tension filled the air.

"So, what's the deal, Anna? You've suddenly turned into a lesbian?" Henry's voice cracked on the last word.

Anna shifted in her seat, and Kylie moved closer.

"What are you talking about?" Anna replied.

"I get a text from this lovely thing," he said, motioning in Kylie's direction, "and the next thing I know, we are meeting at the diner, and she is telling me to leave you alone, and now the two of you are *together?*" His words tumbled out.

Anna stood and walked into the kitchen. Henry and Kylie stared at each other. Anna filled the teapot with water and turned the burner on. She opened the cabinet, grabbed three mugs, and set them on the counter. Taking a deep breath, she returned to the living room entrance.

"What does it matter to you, anyway? You are not a part of my life anymore. What makes you think you can just waltz in here and pick up where you left off?

Speaking of which, need I remind you it was *you* who left *me*? *You* left *me*, and you shouldn't have come back."

"Hear, hear!" Kylie chimed in, clapping her hands.

"As for you—" She turned to Kylie. "—you had no right touching my phone and contacting him. This is none of your business!"

Kylie stood and walked to Anna. "You are my business, and you know it. We are in this together."

"You keep making comments about 'us' or 'being together,' but we've never even had a conversation about 'us,' have we, Kylie?" She stepped around Kylie and sank into the couch.

"Anna, think about that night…"

Anna's face flushed. "Wait. Stop. It didn't mean…I made a mistake. I drank too much. You drank too much. It was confusing. I, I don't even know what to think anymore."

****

Anna

Anna's cell phone broke the tension. Her jazzy ringtone blared from the next room. She rose from the couch and headed back to the kitchen. The moment she reached for her phone, it stopped ringing. She felt the weight of the situation. Her thoughts raced. Grabbing the edge of the countertop, she steadied herself as she began swaying. Her migraines were increasing. She'd already had several so far this month, and she knew stress made them worse. Then again, who *didn't* have stress? Life was full of it. As she stood trying to collect herself, her vision became cloudy, then dimmed until everything was a dull gray. If she was getting a migraine, she often didn't get an aura until after the pain hit; sometimes, she didn't have any aura at all. Only a searing, stabbing pain starting at the base of her skull and slithering its way around her temples and forehead. She needed to grab some aspirin. Maybe if she caught it early enough, she wouldn't have to take her prescription. Maybe if she mixed aspirin with ibuprofen and took it with a big cup of coffee, her cocktail would be enough to ward off the pain.

She leaned against the counter and rubbed her eyes, waiting for her vision to clear. Voices rose in an argument from the other room. Yet their words faded. As she stumbled to sit at the kitchen table, the cup nearest her tipped over. Reaching out to catch it, she floundered in the darkness. Her cheery kitchen disappeared from her sight as she leaned into the silent blackness. The next thing she knew, she was on the couch, covered in her grandmother's afghan. Two sets of eyes peered at her as she blinked hers open.

"Are you okay?" Henry asked.

"Move out of the way. I'll take care of her. Anna, how do you feel?" Kylie smoothed Anna's hair off her forehead.

"What happened?"

"I'm not sure, but I think you blacked out or something. We heard a cup break, and when we came into the kitchen, a teacup was on the floor, and you were slumped against the table. Do you want us to call an ambulance?" Henry's phone was in his hand, waiting for her cue.

"No. I'm fine. It's just a migraine." She sat up and swung her legs to the floor. "Look, I can't deal with all of this right now. My head is killing me. I'm gonna rest.

Henry, I'll call you tomorrow. Please leave. I've got to lie down."

Kylie reached for her arm and helped her up. Leading her down the hall she tucked her into bed and pulled the curtains closed.

When she returned to the living room, Henry was still there. He was sitting on the couch. He waited until she sat, then stood and headed for the door. As he eased past her, Kylie grabbed his arm.

"Don't think you can ruin this for me. For *us*. We have a good thing going, and I don't need *you* to come in here and mess it all up." Kylie preceded him to the door and opened it for him, motioning for him to exit. "Good riddance."

He opened his mouth but remained silent. She slammed the door behind him. Kylie grabbed the broom from the hall closet and marched into the kitchen. She bent to clean up the broken shards of ceramic. Picking up a large piece of the broken cup, she closed her fist around it. A small trickle of blood seeped through her fingers as she smiled.

Chapter 12

Anna

The next morning Anna stood at the kitchen sink, leaning forward to stretch the small of her back. The leaves were beginning to change, and she smiled at the bright orange and red peeking out. She felt a warm, gentle hand on her shoulder.

"Want me to rake?" Kylie asked with a grin.

"Nah, it's too soon in the season." Anna gave a small chuckle. "If I wait long enough, they blow into the neighbor's yard."

"Oh, you're a bad girl," said Kylie, grabbing Anna's hand. Anna started to pull away, but Kylie held tight, and Anna let her. "Why didn't you tell me Henry was here?"

"Honestly, I gave up thinking he would even show up again. I mean, I haven't seen him in almost a year. I haven't heard from him. Then out of the blue, *poof*! He shows back up." Anna turned and grabbed a mug from the cupboard. "Coffee?"

"Please. Yeah, I mean, it's pretty random…showing up here like this. I mean, do you want to be with him again? I thought you and I had a good thing starting?" Kylie turned Anna toward her and looked straight into her eyes. "It wasn't just a drunken night, right, Anna? Tell me it meant more than that."

Anna stared back at her, softening her gaze. "I don't know what to think, Kylie," she whispered. "I was raised to think it's wrong. It wasn't an option. I guess I always assumed I was *supposed* to be with a man…"

Kylie grabbed her and hugged her tight.

"I knew it!" She laughed.

Anna wriggled out of the hug, holding Kylie at arm's length.

"It's not as easy as all that. I don't know what I want right now, Kylie. I mean, just cuz it *felt* good doesn't make it right. Also, not for nothing, but you need help. I keep finding blood on the towels, Kylie. What the heck? I mean, what happened to your hand this time? Why is it bandaged this morning? And don't give me some stupid story. How dumb do you think I am? Are you even taking your medications? Even if I wanted to be in a relationship with a woman, I don't know if I could handle this kind of responsibility." She drained the last of her coffee. "You need to get your shit together, Kylie. And now, with Henry here—"

"Wait, Henry? Why is *he* a factor?" Kylie interrupted.

"I'm not sure he is, but we were together for a long time, and we have a history. It's complicated."

"It doesn't have to be complicated. You may have a history, but we can have a *future*," Kylie replied.

"Then you better start working out some stuff and taking your meds and getting some help before we can even consider anything else," Anna said, gesturing toward Kylie's bandaged hand.

****

A few days passed with no word from Henry. As

Anna was pouring herself a cup of coffee, she noticed a bottle of Kylie's pills on the counter. Kylie wasn't home, and she'd been relishing the quiet. Grabbing the bottle, she read the label and set it down again. Lithium. Pretty potent stuff. *It better help*, she thought, setting the bottle back down. She carried the cup of coffee back to her bedroom with her and began searching through her closet to pull together an outfit for work. Tuesdays were her late days, and she enjoyed being able to take her time. Her favorite client was coming, and she was looking forward to a good discussion. Since Anna's mother's passing, Helen had taken her under her wing. They'd met a few times outside of the salon. Anna smiled as she remembered the last time they went out for lunch. She complained about Kylie's constant need for attention and Anna's own confusion about the nature of their relationship. Helen's wisdom put things in perspective.

"Love doesn't always require a definition. It comes in all forms, and not always when we are ready for it."

Anna laughed it off, asking if it came from a greeting card.

Helen chuckled. "No, just from life. Some of my closest friends came into my life when I wasn't even looking. They eased their way right into my heart."

Anna snapped back to the present.

"Ugh. Where is it?" She began rummaging through her closet faster. Setting her coffee down on the dresser, she opened drawer after drawer. No sweater. "I swear, Kylie, you better not have gotten into my clothes." She walked down the hall to Kylie's door. Uneasiness swept over her as she opened the door and walked in. The room was a mess. The bed was unmade, and clothes were strewn all over the floor. Among the rumpled mess lay her favorite purple sweater. She brought it to her nose and abruptly pulled it away. It reeked of cigarette smoke. She stormed out of the room and threw it in the hall hamper. Kylie was going to hear about this.

****

On the way to work, Anna stopped at the florist around the corner. She liked running into Daisy's to pick up a small bouquet to brighten her workspace. Today she wanted something special for Helen. When she came in three weeks ago for her wash and set, she looked pretty worn out. Anna knew the anniversary of her husband's death was coming up; maybe this would help cheer her.

"Mornin', Anna. How are you?" Daisy always seemed cheerful, even on the dreariest of days.

"I'm good. How have you been? How's business?"

"It's been good. Ever since our website started up, business is booming! I'm actually looking to hire someone part-time. I can't keep up with the hours."

"Really? That's great! How soon are you hiring?"

"Are you looking for work?" Daisy smiled at her.

"No, not me. But I might know someone." *Maybe this is a chance to get Kylie away from dancing.* "Do you have an application I can grab for her?"

"Of course!" Daisy bent down below the counter and grabbed the form.

Chapter 13

Kylie

Kylie bent down and re-tied her shoelace. She was on a mission to start running again. Insomnia had been her bedfellow for the past four nights, and she was still bleary-eyed even with three cups of coffee in her system. Looking bedraggled in her line of work wasn't an option. Besides, the late-night eating was beginning to catch up with her. Her favorite pair of jeans stretched beyond a sexy cling. She felt more like a stuffed sausage than an exotic dancer.

Hat pulled low over her eyes, she eased her way down the street. It was one thing to grab the attention of men who were paying to watch her but quite another to have strangers leering at her while she huffed her way to the inexplicable high she so craved.

Since her attack, she changed her routine, so she now ran as the school buses were dropping the kids off at school in the morning. Sticking to a route near the school parking lot made her feel a bit more secure.

"Kylie!" A male voice interrupted her solitude.

She turned and was alarmed to see Henry jogging her way.

"What the hell are you doing here?" She kept her pace, forcing him to speed up to meet hers.

"Will you slow down?" He huffed. "I stopped by to

see if you guys were home, and I saw you outside."

"Anna's at work." She kept running.

"Slow down. Geez! Stop for a second, will ya?"

Kylie abruptly stopped, causing him to stumble and self-correct. She turned to glare at him.

"What do you want?"

"To talk. Can we talk for like five minutes?"

"Why?" She started to jog in place.

"I need to know how this happened." Henry reached toward her shoulder, but Kylie pulled away.

"How *what* happened? Me and Anna?" She laughed. "It's easy. She needed someone to love, and I showed up." Henry's face looked pinched as if it was more than simply the morning sunlight clouding his vision. Kylie began stretching. Bending down to touch her toes, she allowed her low V-cut T-shirt to hang open. He looked away.

"But she likes men. I mean, she did like them anyway," he muttered.

Kylie clasped her arms behind her neck, arched her back, and let out a sigh.

"People change."

"No. Not Anna. Look, I made a mistake, a huge mistake. But I need her back. I don't know what I was thinking. No, I wasn't thinking." He corrected himself. "And you, you just met her. You don't even really know her. Not the way I do."

"I know her better than you think I do." She glared at him.

"You think you do. But you don't. Look, I don't know what your deal is, or how you turned her, or whatever, but you need to back off and let me deal with this," Henry said.

"I'm not keeping you from her." She laughed. "Did you ever even consider that she might not want to be with you?"

Henry let out a long sigh. His gaze darted toward her. She could feel the sorrow and regret pulsating from him, but she didn't care. Anna was hers. He turned and sauntered away.

****

Anna

The small bouquet of orange and white carnations was perched on the edge of Anna's counter. She scooped up a handful of sterilized combs and arranged them in the oversized mug she picked up during her last trip to Toronto. She found it in a second-hand store off Bloor Street. In rainbow letters, it said *Hairdressers do it with style!*

She and Henry used to go to Toronto every year. They stayed at a little bed-and-breakfast in the Annex neighborhood and loved going into all the shops along Bloor and Spadina.

The last time they'd been there was right after she'd told him she was pregnant. Henry was so excited he started shopping for baby clothes immediately. He was convinced they were going to have a little girl. *He was right. But she slipped away from us.* Anna blinked hard and cleared her throat. She slid the flowers to the center of her workspace and greeted her first customer of the day.

"Good morning, sweetie!" Mrs. Lampfry chirped. "You look a bit pale, my dear. Are you okay?"

"Good morning. Yes, you know, allergy season," Anna replied, sniffling. "Must be the pollen."

After exchanging small pleasantries, Anna fell into the mind-numbing routine of setting Mrs. Lampfry's hair.

The rest of the workday was a blur. Anna managed to get through it, forcing herself to make cheerful conversation with her clients. During her lunch break, she sat on the bench outside and began unwrapping her sandwich. It was a beautiful fall day. The leaves started changing a few weeks ago and were at the peak of colorful perfection. Soaking in the hues reminded her of watching that famous artist with the afro performing TV magic with his creations. Pressing her sore back against the bench, she closed her eyes and inhaled. A shadow passed in front of her, and she blinked open to see Henry standing there. She met his gaze and was surprised at the electricity in the air.

For a few seconds, her brain forgot that almost ten months had gone by. Despite her best effort not to, she smiled at him, and her heart sped up as they made eye contact. Then a wave of hurt and anger washed over her. Her brows wrinkled and her smile erased.

"What are you doing here?"

"Coming to see you," he replied, sitting down beside her.

"I need to get back to work soon. I have a two o'clock client." Anna wrapped up her food, hoping Henry would get the message that she wasn't interested in chatting.

"Look, Anna," he began.

"No, you look. I don't know what you expect from me, but having you show up after all this time. It's crazy. It doesn't make sense. I've finally moved on."

"Have you?" He took her hand in his and kissed

her knuckles.

Anna snatched her hand away. "I've got to go." She stood and shoved her remaining food into her crumpled paper bag.

"I know I don't deserve your forgiveness. I know that. I was hoping you would consider giving it anyway?"

Anna wanted to walk away. She wanted to continue to show him how much he'd hurt her. But her feet were made of lead.

"I'm sorry. I'm so sorry." He reached out to stroke her hair, pulling her into an embrace. They sat in silence for a few minutes until Anna moved away from him.

Her mind raced as she tried to figure out what to say next.

"I…I know you're mad, and hurt, and all sorts of things. You should be. I'm sorry. I am so sorry I hurt you. I wish I could take it all back." He paused and waited for her response. When he got none, he continued.

"I shouldn't have just left. It was wrong. You certainly didn't deserve it. After all you did for me…" His voice cracked, and he cleared his throat. Anna locked eyes with him.

"Why did you do it?" she whispered. "Why did you leave?"

Henry bent forward as if his stomach ached. He cradled his head in his hands and sighed.

"I don't know. I mean, it was wrong of me. I guess I couldn't look at you without thinking of what we lost. It hurt too much. I felt guilty, like I didn't protect you, and…her."

Tears started to trickle down Anna's face. As much as she tried to hold it in, a small sob escaped from her lips, followed by a low moan. She felt like the hollow place inside of her she had been trying to guard for so long was being pulled and stretched and squeezed. It was excruciating. She bowed her head as her body shook.

Henry slid closer, so their thighs were touching. She could feel the heat through the worn softness of his jeans. She continued to sob. He paused for a few seconds before he put his arm around her shoulders and drew her against him. Falling into the familiar groove between his neck and shoulder, she breathed in the scent of home. He held her until her breathing slowed, and she gently pulled away.

"Things are so different now. There's a lot you don't know," she mumbled.

"You mean about Kylie?" He cleared his throat, pausing a beat. "So, tell me."

"Now's not the time. My next client will be here any minute. I've got to get back to work."

"Will you at least let me take you out to dinner tonight?"

Anna stood and smoothed her sweater. "Text me the name of the restaurant, and I'll meet you there at seven." Her mind was swirling with objections, but her heart wasn't listening.

****

The next few days, Anna made every attempt to avoid Kylie. Luckily, it wasn't too hard, as Kylie was working overtime. She would make a few hurried appearances where she would run, grab a shower and bite to eat, and head back out. Although she didn't like to admit it, Anna was enjoying her time with Henry. They'd seen each other for the past three days. Tonight, he was taking her out to dinner again. She was leaning over the bathroom sink, putting her contacts in, when she heard the door slam open. She bristled as she heard Kylie muttering while heading down the hallway. Without warning, the bathroom door swung open as Kylie threw herself in front of the toilet, flung it open, and vomited. Anna backed up and headed out the door.

"Geez, are you okay?" She clamped her hand over her face and stared down at the floor. Kylie motioned for her to leave and began vomiting again.

Anna rushed into the kitchen and grabbed a can of ginger ale, pouring Kylie a glass. She set it down on the kitchen table as Kylie stumbled in and sat. Her face was pale, and her eyes looked a bit glassy.

"Do you have a fever? Do you think it's the flu?"

Kylie stared up at her and shook her head.

"Food poisoning?"

Kylie cried.

"What's going on? Do you want to lie down? I know I get weepy when I'm sick."

"No." Kylie's voice was sharp. Tears trickled down her face. "I'm not sick. I'm pregnant."

Chapter 14

Anna

Anna stared at her for a moment, too stunned to speak. It felt like time applied the brakes, like being in a car accident, where everything moves in slow motion for a moment. The impact is coming. There's no escape. Kylie sank to the floor. Her body shook as she sobbed. Crouching beside her, Anna placed her hand on her back and traced small circles along her shirt. Kylie burrowed into Anna's chest and squeezed her tightly.

In between sobs, Anna could hear, "What am I gonna do?"

Anna rocked back on her heels, unable to continue holding Kylie while still crouching. She eased her butt down to the floor and put her arm around Kylie's shoulder. Their heads bent toward each other as Kylie continued to cry. Finally, when silence started to fill the the space between them, Anna spoke up.

"Kylie, I hate to ask this, but do you know who the father is?"

"It's one of those assholes." She grabbed the hairbrush off the side of the sink and started to smash it against her head. It was as if Kylie had morphed into another person. Her eyes were wild and dark. They reminded Anna of a feral cat.

"Stop! Kylie, stop it!" Anna lunged for the brush

and snatched it from her hand. Pulling her into a bear hug, they rocked while Kylie sobbed. A few minutes later, Anna extricated herself from the embrace to grab some toilet paper off the roll. She handed a wad of the paper to Kylie. After blowing her nose and wiping the remnants of mascara from beneath her eyes, Kylie cleared her throat.

"I can't raise a baby."

"Okay," began Anna.

"But I don't believe in abortion." Kylie stared at her.

"You have time to decide."

"I'm trapped. I *don't* know what to do!" Tears trickled down her cheeks again.

Anna slid her hand into Kylie's and led her down the hall and into the living room. Guiding her to the couch, she placed the afghan over her as they sat down together.

"Okay, you say you don't believe in abortion, but if this pregnancy happened when those guys…"

"So what? I mean, it doesn't matter. A baby shouldn't have to die because her father was an asshole!" She pulled the afghan up over her head and began slowly rocking back and forth.

"All right. I get that, but maybe—I dunno, maybe you should talk to someone else about your options. I mean, like, maybe your counselor?"

Snorting and pulling the afghan down, wrapping it tighter around herself, she replied, "Why? So she can put me on more antidepressants? Oh shit! What about these meds I'm taking?"

"Let's call and set up some appointments for you, okay?"

"Okay." Kylie slumped back against the couch and grabbed the remote.

Anna reached for the telephone and began scrolling.

****

"She's pregnant." Anna's voice sounded hollow. She pulled a small bottle of pills from her purse, popping two and taking a sip of her iced coffee.

Sheila looked at her, remaining silent.

"Why is God so cruel?" Anna tucked her feet underneath her, pulling a throw pillow onto her lap.

"What do you mean by cruel?" Sheila paused. When she was met by silence, she continued. "It sounds as though you are having a hard time with this news."

Anna nodded. Her eyes filled with tears. "I mean, and I'm not sure I should be divulging this, but she was raped. And now, she's pregnant." Her hand flew to her mouth as she tried to cover a sob. She cried, her hands covering her face as the tears slipped down her cheeks onto her shirt. When she finished, she looked up at Sheila for some words of comfort.

"Would it be okay if I come and sit next to you on the couch?"

She nodded. Sheila stood and crossed over to the couch. They sat silently for a moment as the sun outside the window peeked in, casting a strip of light onto the coffee table in front of them.

"What are you feeling right now?" Sheila whispered.

"I mean, it's so completely unfair, right? Being raped is horrible enough, but having a child as a result of such violence? It's like the universe is punishing her or something." Her eyes filled again, and she swallowed her feelings down the best she could.

Sheila sighed. "I wonder if this pregnancy is bringing up some feelings of loss for you?"

Another sob escaped as Anna nodded. The vulnerability of the situation made it hard for her to look Sheila in the eyes. She felt exposed, and she preferred to wear a cloak of physical pain over actually feeling her emotions.

"Yeah." Sheila passed her another tissue. "None of it seems fair, right?"

The women sat side by side, both staring at the pattern on the table before them. Anna noticed the ticking of the clock on the wall. She watched the red second hand move around the circle, waiting until it reached the top.

"I know I should be feeling bad for Kylie. I mean, it's a horrible situation. I can't even imagine what I would do. But all I can think about is my own pain, my own loss. I thought I was over it, ya know?"

"It sounds like you had an expectation of yourself to get over a very significant loss. And now, this news from Kylie is triggering some intense emotions for you?"

"Yeah." Anna hiccuped. A laugh bubbled to the surface. "I'm sorry, I don't know why I laughed."

"It's okay. You don't need to apologize for anything. There is no right or wrong way to mourn. And," she continued, "there is no right or wrong timeline for mourning. Sometimes, it creeps back into our lives without warning."

Anna squeezed the bridge of her nose. "I know. I know. But it hurts so much. I don't like feeling my feelings." She shoved the growing wad of used tissues into her purse, closing the window of vulnerability for the moment. "Ugh. My head is killing me."

Sheila jotted something down in the notebook in front of her. It always irked Anna that Sheila took notes. She understood it, of course. But often, Anna wondered what exactly she took the time to write down, and why? What was significant enough to warrant her scribbling? She was too polite to ask, but allowed herself the brief annoyance.

Sheila interrupted her thoughts. "Have you been journaling?"

Anna shifted in her seat, feeling the weight of her therapist's disappointment as an itchy woolen cloak across her shoulders. "Not really. I know I should be. It does seem to help."

"Does it? What about journaling seems to help?" Sheila asked.

"Um, I guess it just helps to get stuff off my chest instead of carrying it around with me all day long."

"Well, that sounds like a good thing. Is there anything that's standing in the way of you journaling on a more regular basis?"

"Not really. I just haven't made time for it. I've been having so many migraines lately, that when I'm resting, I usually just crash on the couch and binge-watch TV. I don't usually feel like writing."

Sheila looked down at her notes again, then asked, "I wonder what it would be like if you were to journal during a time when you're actually feeling fairly good? I mean, what if your migraines are your brain's way of forcing your body to slow down? What if you beat your brain to it and took a few minutes to write about whatever emotions you are experiencing before they build up?"

"I could try." Anna nodded. "I guess I never really thought about my migraines forcing me to slow down. It makes sense, though."

Is my brain creating pain just to divert my attention from feeling my feelings? She pushed away the heavy thought and smiled politely at Sheila. Her notebook was now closed. Their time for today was up.

Chapter 15

Kylie

The psychiatrist sitting in front of her seemed like a bit of a cliché. Impeccably dressed in an expensive navy suit, with a crisp white shirt and a red bow tie, he walked out into the waiting room. Kylie resisted the urge to laugh. His jet-black hair could have only come from a bottle, and his oversized plastic-rimmed glasses added a bit of flair to the ensemble.

"Miss Teeter, please follow me."

Paperwork littered the office. Stacks of files were piled so high, several of them looked quite precarious. Dr. Stevens sat in a high-backed leather chair. Kylie was across from him in a faded blue armchair. A vat of antibacterial hand gel, a box of tissues, and a vase of wilted flowers were beside her on a glass table. The walls hosted an eclectic collection of art. A few looked like crudely drawn children's pieces, featuring families or houses with sunny lawns. The one that stood out was a painting of a man screaming and holding his head, his face wracked with torment. Above his wild hair, about a dozen fiery-red question marks appeared. She brought her attention back to the man sitting across from her.

"How are you, Miss Teeter? Why don't we start with you telling me what brings you here today?"

"Well, my regular psychiatrist is out of town, and

the office said you had a cancellation and I could come in today."

"Yes, I read Dr. Frederic's notes, and I understand you have been taking lithium for about two months now. How have things been going for you? How have you been feeling?"

"It's all right, I guess. I mean, I feel kind of fuzzy, and I dunno—like flat?"

"Could you tell me more? You say you feel flat? What does flat mean?" Kylie watched him as he scribbled down notes in her file.

"I guess I feel like I'm numb?"

"All right. That can be a complaint of lithium. How would you say your memory has been?"

"Look, I'm gonna cut straight to the chase. I found out I'm pregnant, and I don't wanna totally screw up this baby. So, I'm here to find out what I'm supposed to do."

"I see."

"Is lithium safe?"

"Well, lithium is a Class D drug, which is not recommended during pregnancy. However—"

Kylie interrupted. "Okay, so what do I do? Just stop cold turkey? Cuz, at the hospital, I was warned not to."

"I'll be honest with you, Kylie. It hasn't been very long since your hospitalization. In reading over Dr. Frederic's notes from last month, he felt that your mood was starting to stabilize. I don't recommend going off your medication. But we may want to consider switching you to a different class of drug."

"What does that mean?"

"Well, we could try switching you over to an

antidepressant. A mood stabilizer like lithium is not the best option during pregnancy. We might consider Wellbutrin, which is a Class B drug."

"Okay, fine. I'll try it, I guess. But can't I stop taking drugs altogether?"

"You do have that right. However, based on what I read about your hospitalization, I wouldn't want to take a chance of having you relapse. Having another manic episode would not be good for a baby either."

Kylie picked up the bottle of sanitizer near her and squeezed out a generous amount. "Okay. Fine. Let's do it."

Chapter 16

Anna

Kylie wasn't home by the time Anna arrived from work. She hurried inside and locked herself in the bathroom. Stripping and stepping into the shower, she closed her eyes as the hot water cascaded over her body. This week had been especially stressful, and her aches and pains were lingering. The steady stream helped loosen the tightness in her lower back. *Maybe I should treat myself to another massage.* Her fingers probed the knot at the base of her skull. Pushing into it, she could feel a roll of muscle tighten as pain shot through her left eyebrow. She pushed harder even though the pain felt blinding for a second. As she continued to press, the pressure in her head dissipated. *Hmmm.* She tried the other side and was surprised to feel some relief there, too. Letting go, she tipped her head back under the water, mentally reviewing her wardrobe.

****

Henry arrived at Bruschetta's at seven. Anna was already there, waiting for him in the vestibule. The place was packed, so she arrived ahead of time and put her name on the waiting list.

"Let's go over to the bar and kill time," Henry suggested. They squeezed into a small space and stood by the edge of the bar, waiting to order a drink.

"You look beautiful." Henry winked at her.

She blushed. It had been a while since anyone complimented her. After he abandoned her, she took little interest in her appearance. Tonight, however, she pulled out a new sweater and paired it with her favorite black skirt and heels. The sweater was an impulse buy and cost more than she wanted to admit. It was a creamy-beige cashmere with shimmering tiny white sequins lining the scoop neck. It made her feel beautiful, which helped in justifying the cost. Her blonde hair was pulled up into a twist and secured with a silver clasp.

Soon, she was sipping her wine, and her brain and body grew comfortably numb.

Once their table was ready, Henry walked behind her and scooted ahead at the last minute to pull out her chair. *He was always such a gentleman.* Anna sat and began fidgeting with the zipper of her purse.

"Thanks for agreeing to come out with me."

"It's okay. I mean, we all have to eat, right?" She giggled. *Am I getting a bit tipsy already?* Anna glanced at her wineglass and was surprised to see she had almost finished her drink.

"More wine?" Henry smiled.

"No. Gosh, no. I think I drank this way too fast already."

"You were always a bit of a lightweight." He laughed.

"Oh, like you should talk! I'm surprised you even ordered wine. You have the lowest tolerance of any guy I know!" She giggled again.

"Oh, so do you know a lot of lushes?"

"Hardly." She snorted. "Although, I'm starting to feel like one. I hope they come and take our order soon. I think I need to get some food into me."

"Want an appetizer?"

"I wouldn't say no."

When the waitress arrived, Henry ordered a shrimp cocktail and more wine. As soon as it arrived, Anna helped herself.

"Anna, I want to apologize again for hurting you so much. I don't have a good excuse for leaving you. I guess it was my way of dealing with my own pain, but it was immature of me. I'm so sorry."

"I know you are. I sort of hated you for a long time. And I can't say I understand, but I do believe you're sorry. It's just, and I'm not saying this to give you false hope or anything, but how could I ever trust you again to not *leave* when things get tough?" Anna sighed, pushing her plate away from her.

Henry set his fork down. "I don't know. Even if I gave you my word I would never do that again, I don't know how to prove myself to you. All I know is I should have never left. I couldn't see anything except for how much I was hurting. But after I went back home to my parents, and I started looking back at the whole situation, I realized we needed each other more than ever."

Anna remained silent. Her mind was buzzing. *What is it I want? How can he show up, come back all of a sudden and expect us to get back together? I do still love him, and we were happy together, but what if he leaves me again? I can't go through that pain again. And what do I do about Kylie?*

****

Kylie

Kylie sat on the cold, hard examination table. The paper beneath her crinkled each time she moved. The tiny room was freezing, which annoyed her since they made her strip out of her cozy sweater and jeggings to put on this stupid paper-thin gown. Before she could respond to the quick knock on the door, it opened, and a stately woman walked in. She reminded Kylie of her eighth-grade math teacher. She hated that teacher. A terrified-looking resident accompanied her. Her cheap clipboard was stuffed with pamphlets.

"Okay, Kylie." She sat down opposite the table and peered at her from under her wire-rimmed glasses. "Your pregnancy test is positive. So, we need to do a quick internal exam to make sure everything looks good. Can you lie back for me for a moment?"

Kylie lowered her back against the frigid surface and closed her eyes.

****

Anna

By the time the meal ended, Anna was pleasantly full. Her head still felt a bit fuzzy from the wine. Henry paid, and together they walked to the parking lot.

"Where are you staying, anyway?"

"The Radisson, near the airport."

"Oh." Anna picked at her cuticle. "How long are you staying?"

"That depends on you."

A million thoughts swirled through Anna's mind. *Am I setting myself up to be hurt? Does he deserve to be let back into my heart? Should I just walk away?*

She looked into his clear blue eyes. They were so

familiar. Full of anguish, fear, and yes, she could still recognize it, love.

"Does the Radisson have an indoor pool?"

"Yep, sure does. Feel like swimming?"

She smiled, ignoring her brain and following her heart.

Chapter 17

Kylie

"So far, everything looks good, Kylie. You're about ten weeks pregnant. I'd like to schedule an ultrasound. It's routine. Do you have any questions?"

"What about this medication I'm supposed to be taking?"

"The Wellbutrin? Well, I've worked with several mothers who have had to stay on their meds throughout their pregnancy. My feeling is it would be more detrimental for you to be off your medications. You should stay on it. There are always risks involved to the fetus when the mother is on medication, but it is fairly low with this drug."

"What about dancing?"

"Dancing?" The doctor adjusted her glasses.

"I'm, um, an exotic dancer. I mean, will dancing like—hurt the baby?"

"Oh, well—no. But you will start showing soon. I'm assuming you may need to find a different line of work, temporarily." She smiled and busied herself with Kylie's chart.

****

Anna

Anna climbed out of bed, pulling the blanket

around her. Rushing into the bathroom, she started the water for a shower. It was almost eight a.m., giving her under an hour to get to work. She would either have to wear the same clothes or run home to change. Neither option seemed very appealing. She showered using the tiny bar of soap and travel shampoo. As she opened the bathroom door, she was surprised to see Henry sitting on the edge of the made bed. He stood and held out her jacket.

"Leaving so soon?" He grinned.

"I've gotta get to work. I'm going to run home and change first." She blushed. "This"—she wiggled her finger motioned toward the bed—"does not mean we're back together."

Henry stared at her and opened his mouth to speak. Then, he surprised her with a coy smile.

"I'm serious!" she protested.

He smiled again and nodded. Grabbing her purse off the floor and swiping the jacket from his hand, she pecked his cheek and turned to leave.

"See you tonight?"

Exasperated, she pulled the door open. "Maybe."

Chapter 18

Anna

"Where have you been?" Kylie's harsh tone erupted as soon as Anna walked into the kitchen. The table was strewn with papers and pens. Kylie's chin was propped on her upturned palm as she sat slumped at the table.

Anna cleared her throat and ignored the question. "What are you doing?"

"Applying for jobs. I'm gonna guess a pregnant stripper isn't high on the sexy list," she grumbled.

"So, you've decided to keep the baby?"

"If you mean, have I decided not to *kill* it, then yes. I mean, it's not her fault her sperm donor was a rapist."

"Her?" Anna sat down at the adjacent chair and tried to resist smiling. "Do you already know it's a girl?"

Kylie stopped writing. "No, but I just have a feeling. I guess I can find out in a few more weeks for sure."

Anna regarded her. Her black hair was flat and greasy. Her thin red tank top and ripped black leggings left nothing to the imagination. She certainly wasn't shy about her body, and her clothes always clung in all the right places. Still painfully thin, it didn't seem as if an actual baby had any room to grow. Anna could still remember the taste of her skin on her lips. *What was I thinking? Did I imagine it all?* Anna never considered herself the adventurous type, but she was curious to explore when it came to Kylie.

"What's wrong?"

"Huh? Oh, nothing." Anna started to straighten the piles in front of her. "I guess I'm worried about you. How are you feeling?"

"Well, I've only thrown up four times so far today."

"Geez, that sucks! Want some ginger ale or something?"

"We're all out."

"I'll go get you some." Before she could object, Anna slipped out the door, leaving behind the feeling of desperation clinging to the air surrounding Kylie.

Chapter 19

Anna

It was difficult, but Anna managed to limit her time alone with Kylie during the week. She left the application for Daisy's flower shop on the table with a note explaining she was picking up a few extra shifts at the salon. She did agree to work one extra night this week, in addition to Saturday. In reality, she was spending the rest of her time outside of work with Henry. He was still staying at the hotel, and it was no secret his time here was limited.

"I have to head back home tomorrow, Annie. I wish I could stay longer, but I have to get back to work. Plus, my niece is getting baptized on Sunday."

"Brianna had another baby?"

"Yep, she and Scott got married last year. It's his. They named her Unique."

"Really? Unique, huh? Hmm, well, to each their own."

He grabbed her hand and turned it over. Peeling back her fingers one by one, he kissed her palm. Shivers shot down the length of her spine.

"Annie. I can come back." She looked up at him, alarmed. "I mean it. My job is at a temp agency. I'm not tied down to anything. I want to be here with you."

Waiting had never been one of Anna's strong suits.

She was always reaching for something in life that remained right outside of her grasp. Living in the here and now was a challenge. Her life had been planned out so neatly in the past. Go to school, get married, have a child. With Henry's illness and his past hesitancy to get married, she was always one step behind her dreams.

When they lost the baby, she gave up dreaming. Survival mode was hard enough.

"No," she said with finality. Henry stepped back. She recognized the pained expression. It reminded her of the photos of him as a small boy. His expression filled with innocence and charm. She watched him closely now as his eyes clouded with anger.

"What have we been doing here, Annie?" he whispered.

"I don't know. But I didn't ask for any of this. I thought you were my *person,* Henry. But then you walked away. I don't expect you to pack up your life and come back here now." She started chewing on a ragged cuticle.

"Expect it? I *want* it. Don't you want it too?"

Anna could feel the sting of unfallen tears. "I don't know what I want." She covered her eyes with both hands and sighed. "I know what I wanted. But everything changed when you left."

Circling her with his arms, he buried his face in her hair. She hesitated for a moment before giving in and accepting his warm comfort. When her cell rang, she swore under her breath and wrapped her arms around him in return.

Ignoring it, she stood in his embrace. The phone rang several times before going to voicemail. Then it started ringing again.

He pulled away. "Go ahead and get it."

She pulled it out of her jeans pocket. "It's Kylie. If I don't answer it now, she'll keep calling and calling. Hello?"

"Anna? Can you come home?"

"I'm kind of busy right now. What's up?"

Kylie sobbed. "I'm bleeding. Bleeding is bad, right? I shouldn't be bleeding, right?"

Anna turned away from Henry and whispered into the phone. "You mean from cutting?"

"No! Please come. I'm scared."

"Okay, hang up and call your doctor. I'm on my way."

"What's going on?" Henry followed her to her car.

"I've gotta go. It's Kylie."

"She's a big girl, Anna. Why can't she take care of herself? I mean, this is a serious conversation we're having here."

Opening her door and sliding into the vehicle, she was surprised when Henry got into the passenger seat. She stared at him in silence for a moment. Raising an eyebrow, he shut the door and grabbed for the seatbelt. Anna started the car.

Chapter 20

Anna

She was spotting. The doctor sat with Kylie and Anna and explained spotting sometimes occurred during pregnancy. The blood tests came back fine, and her iron level was good, so they recommended Kylie return home and rest for the remainder of the day. If the bleeding persisted or became heavier, she was to call immediately.

On the way home, Anna was pensive. She drove in silence as Kylie's head lay against the headrest, her eyes closed. Henry stayed with them throughout the doctor's appointment, and they had just dropped him off at his car left in the salon parking lot.

What am I going to do? Do I even want to be with Henry again? And what about everything that happened with Kylie? What does it all mean, anyway? Am I a lesbian? Her mind was so focused on these mysteries she almost ran a red light. She jolted to a stop.

"Geez!" Kylie bolted upright. "Are you trying to kill me?"

"Sorry."

"Are you okay? You don't look so good. Don't get me wrong; you're still *hot*." She placed her hand on Anna's knee.

"Stop."

"What?" She pulled away. "Why? What's going on?"

"Nothing. Let's go home."

"Wait a second. Is this about Henry? I kinda forgot about him for a bit there."

Anna refused to look at her. Her gaze remained transfixed on the road.

"Shit! You're getting back together, aren't you?"

Turning onto their street, Anna sighed. "I don't want to talk about this right now. Besides, you need to rest."

Kylie was crying. As they pulled up to the driveway, she started to open the door before the car completely stopped. "Let me out!"

"Kylie! Wait!" Anna turned off the car and slammed the door behind her as she followed Kylie up the walk. "Stop acting like a whiny little kid. This is why I can't talk to you."

"Why?" Kylie turned. "Because I'm crazy?" She shoved her key into the lock and threw the door open. Anna grabbed the door before it could slam into the doorstop. Closing the door against the now frigid wind, Anna reached for her arm.

"I'm not say—You're not crazy. But you do have *issues.* And you're pregnant."

"Don't you think I have a right to know what's going on? I mean, after the other night…"

"Stop. I'm so confused. I don't know what that night was about. I don't know what to think." Anna flinched as Kylie strode over. Before Anna could stop her, Kylie leaned in and kissed her. Her hands automatically reached for the back of Kylie's head. Her hands tangled themselves in her hair. Petal-soft lips brushed against each other.

"Stop thinking." Kylie breathed.

For a split second, Anna allowed herself to be lost in the seduction of it all. But then, her mind snapped back into action, and she pulled away.

"I can't," she said.

Kylie's arms fell to her sides in defeat. She opened her mouth to speak, but no words emerged.

They stared at each other, and then wordlessly, Kylie turned and left. Her bedroom door clicked shut.

Chapter 21

Anna

Anna was late again. She knew that Henry was inside waiting for her, but she felt as though she was glued to the seat. The sunlight warmed the interior of her car as she sat in silence. Henry's flight was due to leave in less than three hours. They were supposed to meet at their old coffee hangout at three p.m. It was already a quarter after. Her phone had buzzed several times already, but she chose to leave it unchecked on the seat beside her. Even though he had repeatedly promised that he'd be back, she had her doubts. Sadness—sat like a wet lump of clay in her chest. She dug her fingers into the familiar knot in her neck, frustrated that she'd wasted her money on a massage yesterday. Everything was tight and painful again.

A knock at the passenger window startled her. She looked up to see Henry's face peering in at her. Flustered, she unlocked the door, hoping she looked better than she felt. She tried to smile at Henry as he slid in beside her.

"What's wrong? What's going on?"

All of Anna's determination to stay strong melted away as Henry leaned over the middle console and tried to hug her. She started to laugh at the absurdity of the awkward pose, but a sob escaped instead.

"Annie," he whispered. "What is it?"

"I don't know what to do anymore." She sobbed. Unable to fully hug her, Henry settled for rubbing her arm through her wool pea coat. He waited for her to continue.

"I'm so confused. I feel like everything is falling apart."

"What do you mean?"

Anna took a deep, cleansing breath and wiped away her tears. The words tumbled out in a jumble. "It's Kylie. She was raped, and now she's pregnant. You make a sudden reappearance in my life, and now you're leaving again, and…" A single tear slid down her pale cheek. "I think, I think I might be bisexual."

Henry stopped rubbing her arm. He sat back against his seat and turned his face toward the window. Silence filled the small space between them. As he turned to face her, his eyes were full of regret. She resisted the urge to look away. A familiar ache filled her heart.

"Annie. I know I was wrong to leave, and I was gone a long time. But I never stopped loving you. Losing the baby didn't change that. I never stopped loving you, and I never will."

She stared at him, her mouth gaping. "So, you're okay with me? I mean, that I seem to like women too?" She fiddled with her seatbelt buckle, keeping her eyes trained on her lap.

"Honestly, I kinda had my suspicions a few years ago, but it never materialized, so I let it go." He paused. "Annie, do you still love *me*?"

She lifted her chin and stared into his eyes. "Yes."

"I love you too, and I want us to be together again.

Nothing else matters."

Anna wasn't so sure it was that easy.

****

"Kylie, we need to talk." Anna sat down on the couch.

"What now?" she muttered. Stretching her legs out in front of her, she scratched her head, mussing her hair. Anna pushed away from the memory of her hands touching the luscious locks.

"Look, I have some things to say, and I don't think you're gonna be too happy about them."

Kylie slumped back into the cushions and let out a heavy sigh. "Are you getting back with Henry?"

"Yes."

"Is he moving in?"

"Oh, well, he would like to. He went home to take care of some things, but he'd like to come back in a few weeks."

"And what do you want?"

"Honestly? I think that's what I want. And I think we can make it work."

"So, you're kicking me out?" Kylie started to stand, but Anna pulled her back down onto the couch.

"No, Kylie. I'm not. We talked about it, and we'd like you to stay for a while."

"We?" She scoffed. "What about *us*?" Urgency crept into her voice, disguised as a low whine.

"Please don't take this the wrong way, but there is no *us*. I admit I am attracted to you, and I enjoyed our time together, but I want to be with Henry. You and I are friends. I care about you, but as friends. Do you think you can be okay with a platonic friendship?"

"I don't seem to have a choice in the matter, do I?"

she sneered.

"You are welcome to stay if you want, but if it makes you too uncomfortable, I understand. Will you at least think about it?" Anna stood to leave.

"Okay," Kylie replied in a tiny voice.

****

Anna

The next two weeks were quiet. Anna and Kylie moved around the house like strangers. They remained polite and remote. Every night Henry called. They texted each other throughout the day. He was scheduled to move in next week. Kylie was hired at the flower shop, and her first official day of work started tomorrow.

"Anna?" Kylie called from her room. "Can you come here a minute?"

Anna set down her tea and walked toward Kylie's room. From the doorway, the floor wasn't even visible, with clothes strewn everywhere. Empty hangers hung in the closet. Shoes were dumped on the bed.

"What are you doing?" Anna laughed.

"It's not funny! I can't find anything decent to wear for tomorrow! Everything I have either looks too slutty, or it's way too tight!"

"Looks like someone needs to go maternity shopping."

"Very funny. I am *not* wearing maternity clothes!"

"Oh, yeah? Well, I hate to break it to you, but you can only go so long walking around with your jeans unbuttoned." Anna entered the room and started putting items back onto hangers.

"So, I take it you have decided you're gonna keep

the baby?"

"I still don't know. I was thinking about adoption."

Anna's heart thumped. *How could someone carry a baby to term and willingly give her up?* Kylie interrupted her thoughts.

"I don't know quite yet. But I guess I have a little bit of time before I have to decide."

"Well, in the meantime, how about going shopping?"

The women surveyed the chaos of the room again.

"Okay."

****

The last time Anna entered a maternity store was for herself. She and Henry had come together. It was exciting to move into the pregnancy stage where you start showing. Even though her belly was still barely anything more than a tiny baby bump, she had jumped at the chance to join the countless other adorable pregnant women in their chic outfits. The memory was bittersweet and tinged with an intense throb of pain. She tried to focus on Kylie and push the familiar ache toward the back of her heart.

"Does this make my butt look fat?" Kylie joked, spinning around in a pair of maternity jeans. She somehow even managed to make maternity clothes look sexy.

"I bet even when your baby is about to come out, you will still not look fat!" Anna knitted her perfectly arched eyebrows.

Kylie laughed and grabbed a black slinky dress off the rack.

By the time they finished, Kylie had bought three new outfits, several pairs of maternity underwear, two nursing bras, and a pair of jeans. Anna had a stiff neck and a throbbing head. It seemed like she was getting headaches daily now. She was beginning to forget what it was like *not* to have a headache. On the way home, Kylie turned the radio off and placed her hand on Anna's arm.

"Thank you for taking me shopping. I know it must have been hard for you."

"It was a bit, but it was also nice. It's exciting to help you plan and to think about a new little baby growing inside of you."

"Will you and Henry try again?"

"I hope so. We haven't talked about it. He'll be here on Friday. I don't want you to feel uncomfortable having him around."

Kylie twisted her seatbelt, pulling the band away from her belly for a moment. "I'm just glad you're letting me stay."

Chapter 22

Anna

"How did you accumulate so much junk?" Anna exaggerated, straining her back as she lifted another one of his oversized containers.

"I'll have you know this is *not* junk! These are valuable *Flash Gordon* comic books. They're worth money!"

"Really? How much? Maybe we should sell them."

"Very funny." He lifted the box away from her and headed down the basement steps. After unloading the rest of his car, they collapsed on the couch.

"Are you sure Kylie is okay with me moving in? I mean, she's not gonna pull a *Fatal Attraction,* is she?"

"Henry! That's so mean! Just because she has a mental illness doesn't mean she's gonna try to kill you!"

"All right, I know. But I know she still has a *thing* for you. It makes me kinda nervous."

"It surprises me a bit that she's been so calm. I think this new medication is working wonders. By the way, she's picking up a pizza for us on her way home from work."

"Did someone say pizza?" Kylie called as the front door slammed open.

"We're in here!" Anna yelled.

"Hey." Kylie set the box down on the coffee table and gave Anna an awkward hug. She gave Henry a half-hearted smile.

"Thank you so much for the pizza! I'm famished!" Henry opened the box and started to chuckle. "Looks like I'm not the only one!"

"Hey." Kylie snickered as she grabbed a slice for each hand. "I *am* eating for two!"

****

Later that night, the three of them lounged on the couch watching TV. Kylie absentmindedly rubbed her belly. She caught Henry looking at her.

"What?"

"Huh? Oh, nothing. Sorry," he mumbled.

She cleared her throat and stared at the floor. "I'm really sorry about your baby."

Anna turned but said nothing. It was kind for Kylie to acknowledge their loss. She became aware of the loud ticking of the grandfather clock in the hall.

"Thanks," Henry whispered.

"Um, I'm getting kinda tired. I think I'm gonna turn in," Kylie said.

"Oh, okay." Henry cleared his throat. He set the remote on top of the pizza box and smiled at Kylie. "Thanks again for the pizza. Goodnight."

"Goodnight," Anna repeated.

"Night," she replied. Her feet padded down the hallway. They waited until they heard her bedroom door click shut, then snuggled up next to each other on the couch.

****

"Something about her makes me uneasy." Henry spit toothpaste into the sink while Anna sat on the side of the tub, watching him.

"What do you mean?"

"It's like she's a ticking time bomb. I'm afraid to say the wrong thing around her. It kinda feels like I have to walk around on eggshells."

"I think she is doing better lately." She grabbed the floss and got to work.

"I don't think you see the way she looks at you. It's like she's eating you with her eyes."

"Oh, come on, don't you think you're exaggerating just a little bit?"

She bumped him with her hip to get him to move away from the sink and grabbed a tiny paper cup to fill it with water. She rinsed and spit.

"No, I'm serious. I'm sure she wants me out of the way so she can have you all to herself," he chided.

Anna turned to face him. Her butt was up against the sink. She wrapped her arm around his neck and drew him close.

"You've got nothing to worry about. Besides, I told her she can stay for a while, but pretty soon, she's gonna have to start making some sort of plan for this baby. I mean, she mentioned adoption, so she's gonna have to start figuring stuff out. I doubt she's gonna wanna live here forever."

"Let's hope not." He winced as Anna gave him a dirty look. "I wish we could somehow pick up where we left off."

Swallowing her fear of being hurt again, she pulled him closer and brushed her lips across his.

****

Kylie pulled her ear away from the bathroom door and tiptoed away.

Chapter 23

Anna

Morning dawned cold and crisp with a light dusting of snow sprinkling the grass. Anna snuggled under the down comforter, annoyed at the sun peeking through the side of the curtain. She could hear Henry banging around in the kitchen. Pulling her well-worn fleece robe around her body, she followed the aroma of coffee.

"Good morning."

"Hey there, now there's a look for you."

"Shut up." She laughed. "You knew what you were getting into."

"I'm kidding. You're adorable."

"Aww, thanks. Is Kylie up yet?"

Henry grabbed the peppermint mocha creamer from the fridge and handed it over. "I guess she must have left early. Her car is gone."

"Really? I thought she didn't have to work till three today. Hmm. She's not usually an early bird."

"Stop worrying about her so much. Maybe she ran out to get us a dozen fresh donuts." He joked.

"Not likely." Anna slurped her coffee. The morning's first sip was her favorite. She loved the hot rush of caffeine as it trickled down the back of her throat. "Anyway, your new job starts next Monday?"

"Yep. I've got a whole week to goof off before I have to return to the real world."

Anna kissed him as she rushed back past him, letting her fingers graze across his chest. "I'm sorry. I've gotta get ready for work. My first client always arrives a bit early. What time are you going out again tonight?"

"We're meeting at seven." He slathered some of her homemade raspberry preserves on his toast.

Luckily, she made a large batch at the end of the season, so she should have a few jars left before her stash was depleted. She smiled, knowing he would be pleased. He'd always adored her preserves. It was a small thing, remembering this detail about him, but it made her happy to see him enjoy her creation.

"Okay, I should be back a bit after five, so I'll pick up takeout on the way home."

****

Anna hurried off to finish getting ready for work. A pang of jealousy hit her as she thought of Henry's plan to spend the rest of the day puttering around the house. He'd been invited out for drinks with some of his old buddies after they got out of work, so he had the day free. Even though she loved her job, she wished she could stay home today. She popped a few ibuprofen before scribbling a quick note for Henry.

The snow held off, but the bitter bite of winter was still in the air. She resisted the urge to turn on the car's heater before backing out of the driveway. The air would blow icy cold, but she maintained the false hope that it would warm more quickly if it was on. The neighborhood hadn't changed much during Henry's absence. The houses in this tract were all built around the early fifties, and many struggled with the same issues. Most of the front cement steps were starting to crumble. A few of the houses bore tiny wooden porches built over the top of the steps. She remembered asking him to replicate the neighbors' idea with the hopes of improving the look of the outside of the house. Maybe now he'd finally follow through and help her improve the look of the place.

****

After an uneventful day at work, she arrived back home with the food she'd ordered them for dinner. The smell was intoxicating, and it had taken all of her willpower to not break into the package of naan bread at the top of the bag. Henry was ruffling his hair with a damp towel as he walked into the kitchen. She breathed in the clean scent of him as he wrapped his arms around her waist.

"Hey, handsome. I thought you might want a bite to eat before you attack the beer tonight."

"Smells great! Thanks, I'm famished. Let me grab a sweatshirt. Oh, by the way," he said, heading back down the hall, "Kylie never made it back here before her shift."

Anna's heart felt like it dropped into her stomach. Flashes of a worst-case scenario flitted through her imagination. What if Kylie started cutting again? Something didn't feel right. She ran down the hall and flung the door open. The room was dark and stuffy. The icy pang of dread filled her belly as she flipped on the light switch. The bed was made, the dresser neat. It was as if Kylie's presence in the room had been erased.

Anna threw the bathroom door open. The room was empty.

"Henry! She's gone!" Anna shouted.

She ran back down the hall, stopping in their bedroom doorway. "Kylie's gone!"

"Did she leave a note?"

"I don't know. I went to check her room, and all her stuff is gone. I didn't see a note."

He followed her back down the hall. Together they scoured the room, searching for a note. The space looked as if no one had been residing in it for the past several months. Kylie's only remaining presence was in the damp towels hanging on the bathroom rack. Sitting down on the bed, Anna dropped her head into her hands.

"What are we gonna do? What if she's in trouble or something? Where could she have gone?"

Henry sat beside her and began rubbing her back. "Does she have family around here?"

"Not that I know of."

"I hate to say this, I mean, I know how much you care about her, but maybe it's for the best."

Anna bolted upright and glared at him. "How can you suggest I abandon her? She's sick. She needs help!"

"It's not *abandoning* her. She's not a child, and she's not your responsibility. She's an adult. There's only so much you can do."

"But the baby."

"I know. But Annie, as much as you might not want to face this, the baby she's carrying is not ours to worry about."

Anna started to cry. She quickly tried to swipe away the hot tears, but they continued to flow. As Henry wrapped his arms around her, she found it harder to hold the pain in. She rested her throbbing head against his chest. Great heaving sobs escaped in waves as Henry held her tight. She cried for the loss of her own child, never growing up in her love. She cried for the pain of Henry leaving her, for her confused feelings about Kylie, for the tender love she wanted to give her baby. She cried until all the wounded parts of her merged, floating around and enveloping her. She pressed her forehead into Henry's chest, hoping the stabbing between her eyes would subside. Henry held tight and didn't let her go until she pulled away, embarrassed by her lack of control. Aware of her puffy eyes and blotchy face, she looked at the ground, trying to wipe away any remnants of mascara with her sleeve. Henry gently tilted her face back up until they were staring at each other.

"You're not in this alone, Anna. I'm not going anywhere."

She nodded, the metallic taste of doubt filling her mouth. Even as he pulled her back into his arms, her thoughts raced.

Part 2: Kylie

Chapter 24

Kylie

Kylie sped down the highway. Without a destination in mind, she felt the exhilaration of freedom. White-hot anger burned deep inside her, welling up and spilling out in the form of a jagged scream. She pounded her fists on the steering wheel and turned up the radio. Facing her actual feelings was not a favorite pastime; running away from them was much preferred. *They don't want me there? Fine. I don't need them. What's wrong with me anyway? Okay, Kylie, get it together. Enough. Focus. Where are you gonna go? What's your plan?* Kylie laughed out loud. *A plan? When have I ever had a plan for anything? Ha!*

She glanced down at her phone. Five missed calls and two voicemail messages. All but one were from Anna. She swiped her finger across the screen. *Shit! One was from Daisy. I forgot to tell Daisy I wasn't coming back to work. Dear sweet Daisy. Now she's gonna have to find someone else to help around the flower shop.*

Glancing back up, she slammed on the brake to keep from rear-ending the car in front of her. Her unzipped purse flew off the seat beside her, spilling its contents onto the crumb-encrusted floor. Her prescription bottle rattled like a tiny maraca. Her heart was racing. The car ahead of her sped away as her foot remained plastered to the brake. She put the car in park and heaved a sigh of relief. The car behind her beeped and flashed its lights. Kyle rolled down the window and gave the driver the finger. As the car sped past her with an irritated beep, she bent down to retrieve the bottle of medication. Unscrewing the cap, she tipped its contents into her hand. A large pile of pills filled her palm. She regarded the tiny white domes. Smiling, she tossed them out the open window and sped away.

****

Nearly three hours later, nausea settled in her empty stomach. She pulled into the decrepit lot and parked near the front door of the tiny diner. Although the surrounding façade looked aged and crumbled, the place was packed. Music blasted from within. Two men stood nearby, smoking.

Kylie got out and stretched. She ignored the whistles and catcalls and walked into the restaurant.

"Hi there, welcome to Johnny's. How many?"

"Just me."

"Right this way."

Kylie followed the tiny woman to a table in the corner. Her eyes lingered on her svelte body. She couldn't have been over thirty and was in very good shape. Her black pants and pink top hugged her in all the right places. She looked good, and she knew it. Their eyes met, and she smiled. Her tiny crystal nose ring sparkled in the dim light.

"Can I get you something to drink?"

She smiled back at her. "Would you drink it with

me?"

"Excuse me?" the woman whispered, peering around.

"What time do you get off?"

The woman stepped closer and smiled. "Uh, my shift doesn't end till we close tonight."

"And what time do you close?"

"Midnight."

"Hmm, okay, I'll take whatever you have on tap."

The woman cleared her throat. "I'll need to see your ID."

"Seriously?"

"Sorry. Don't be offended, but my manager might be watching."

Kylie pulled her license out of her wallet and laughed again.

"Don't worry. I'm well over twenty-one."

The waitress nodded and studied her ID. "You're from Rochester? What are you doing all the way in Greenville?"

"Honestly, I'm not quite sure yet. I guess I'm looking for a job and a place to stay."

"Oh, well, there is a motel around the corner. It's nothing fancy, but it's clean. It should be. My sister is the cleaning lady over there. They've been looking for a part-time clerk. Like, the kind that sits at the front desk and checks people in. I'll text her and see if she's around tonight."

"Really? Wow. How nice of you. Thanks!"

"No problem. I'll be right back with your drink." The waitress walked away, her chocolate-colored curls bouncing with each step. Kylie glanced around the diner. It was loud and full of a wide variety of people.

The barstools were almost entirely occupied by middle-aged, tired-looking men. Families with rowdy children sat at many of the booths. A young woman sat alone at the table beside her. In front of her stood a plate of fries, a coffee, and a slice of apple pie. She continued munching as she read a thick book. *Maybe I should just stay here. It looks nice enough.* Her thoughts were interrupted as a tall icy glass of beer was set in front of her. Grateful for even a moment of respite, she took a long swig. Her stomach protested, and suddenly the smell was overwhelming. She called for the waitress.

"On second thought, could I have some ginger ale and maybe some soup?"

"Oh, of course. By the way, my sister *is* working tonight. She starts her shift at seven if you wanna run over and meet her. Her name is Dawn. She's good friends with the manager, so if it looks like something you might want to do, she could put in a good word for you."

Kylie was surprised at the kindness of strangers. She'd never been the kind of person who assumed everyone was full of sweet altruism. It seemed like people kept proving her wrong.

By the time Kylie finished eating, it was a quarter after six. She waited to catch the waitress's eye and motioned for her to come over.

"Are you all set?"

"Yes. Thanks again for your help. By the way, I'm Kylie."

"Oh, I thought I introduced myself before. How rude of me! I'm sorry. I'm Aurora."

"Aurora? Such an original name. It's pretty." She paused. "It suits you."

Aurora blushed. Her light brown eyes crinkled slightly at the corners as she smiled again.

"I probably should mention my sister, Dawn, and I are twins."

"Oh! Identical?"

"Yep. We're very much alike." Aurora set the check down along with a tiny scrap of paper with a phone number scribbled on it. "Except, she's straight." She chuckled as she turned and walked away.

****

Kylie spent the next few minutes driving around, checking out her shopping options. There wasn't much to choose from in the tiny town. She settled on a small market connected to the gas station. After parking, she entered the dimly lit establishment. The aisles were wide, sporting shelves of toiletries, snacks, batteries, fishing gear, and food. The entire back wall was a cooler. A magazine rack was overflowing with the latest glossy gossip. She filled her wicker basket up with chocolate, cookies, ramen noodles, crackers, and ginger ale. Pausing near the cooler of beer, she inched her way past the soda and grabbed two chocolate milks. The old man from behind the front counter approached her. He had a long grayish beard and fuzzy white hair that stood out in all different directions. He was slightly stooped and smelled of peppermints and pipe tobacco. He reminded her of a hippy version of Santa. Kylie liked him before he even started to speak.

"Can I be of any assistance to you?"

"Oh, thank you. I guess I'm wondering if you guys sell spoons or bowls or anything like that?"

"No, I'm sorry. But there's a super Walmart about twenty minutes north of here. They've got a bunch of stuff. Oh wait; we do have plastic spoons over there by the coffee machines. Feel free to help yourself to a handful on the way out if ya want."

"Oh, thank you. Well, I guess I'm all set then." She followed him over to the cash register and began unloading her basket.

"I've never seen you around here before. Are you passing through?" He smiled.

"Well, I'm not sure yet. I was going to see if I can find a job."

"Ahh, my niece works over at the motel. I hear they're hiring."

"That's *your* niece? Man, this *is* a small town! I met Aurora at the diner!"

The man's mouth turned up at the corners, and his eyes twinkled. "Yep. I'm their great uncle. Those girls are so sweet! Although Aurora can be a bit saucy." He laughed. Kylie joined him with a chuckle.

"She seemed nice to me."

"Oh, of course she is. But she certainly gave my nephew a run for his money when she was a teenager. Okay, so it will be sixteen dollars and seventy-two cents."

"Here you go. Thanks again for your help. And for the spoons." She grabbed a few before heading out the door.

After locating the local superstore and obtaining the remaining items she needed, Kylie made her way back to town. The Harborview Motel was the only motel in sight, so she assumed it was the one Aurora was referring to. She left all of her new items in the car and walked to the registration area. There was a Help Wanted sign in the window, and Kylie took that as a good omen. The reception area was dim and dank. A clump of dusty fake flowers in a yellow vase adorned the countertop. A brass bell with a ceramic handle in the shape of a mermaid stood next to it. Kylie gingerly picked up the bell and shook it. It jingled loudly. No one came. She tried again, but there wasn't any response. She tried to lean over the counter, but the pressure against her belly was immediately uncomfortable. Exasperated, she walked around behind the counter and looked around. There was a light on in the adjacent room, so she wandered back there. As she stood in the entranceway, a frazzled woman came rushing in.

Despite the blue A-line skirt, white oxford, and navy hair kerchief, she guessed this was Dawn.

"Oh my gosh! I'm so sorry! Did you ring the bell? Have you been waiting long?"

"Oh, it's okay. I was wondering if I could get a room?"

"Sure thing. Let me check you in. My manager is on her dinner break, so bear with me. I'm not the best at the check-in stuff. Our regular desk clerk is on maternity leave."

"Okay." Kylie followed her back to the reception area and walked around to the front of the counter. "Are you Dawn, by any chance?"

She stopped flipping through the binder in front of her and narrowed her eyes as she looked up. "Yes. How did you know?"

Kylie smiled. "I didn't mean to freak you out. It's just…I met your sister at the diner earlier, and she told me you worked here, and they might be hiring?" She held her breath in hopeful anticipation.

"Oh my gosh! Yeah. She texted me. You *want* the job? That would be *amazing*! I mean, it's not up to me, but my manager, Cheryl, will be back soon. Do you wanna check-in, and I'll have her call your room when she gets back?"

"Really? Wow. You guys sure work fast around here. That would be great! Thank you."

"Sure. I mean, we could sure use the help. But like I said, it's not up to me." Dawn handed her the key as she signed in.

****

Anna

"Hey, come on in." Sheila held the door as Anna crossed the threshold, making a beeline for the couch.

"It's been a few weeks since I've seen you. How have you been?"

"I'm okay, I guess. A lot has happened since the last time we met."

Sheila waited for her to continue, sitting down in the chair across from Anna.

"Kylie left."

"Oh? When did she leave?"

"A few weeks ago." Anna tried to measure her words, swallowing down the tears threatening to spill. "At first, I was worried. I mean, I'm still worried, of course. But now, I'm more mad." She laughed as a warm tear escaped down her cheek.

"I don't know why I'm crying. I'm embarrassed. I'm angry. I admit, I feel a little bit crazy. One minute I'm pissed she left like that. After all I did for her. The next minute I'm worried. Where did she go? I don't think she has family around, much less friends. She wasn't exactly an easy friend. But mostly, I'm sad." She swiped another tear away.

"It sounds like you have a lot of different feelings. It makes complete sense. You let her into your life. She was a big part of it. You're not crazy; you're human."

Anna nodded.

"What part about her being gone makes you feel sad?" she asked.

"I mean, I cared about her. Even though Henry is back, I wanted to help her out. We wanted to help her out, ya know?"

"I know." Sheila handed her the box of tissues. "It's okay to feel intense emotions. How has your physical pain been during this time?"

"It's horrible." Anna opened up her purse, popping her pillbox open. "I still have headaches every day. I wake up with them. They get worse throughout the day, and by the time I'm ready to relax after dinner, all I want to do is crawl into bed and sleep so I don't have to feel the pain anymore."

"That does sound horrible. I'm sorry. Have you talked to your doctor about this?"

"Yeah," she replied. "I'm supposed to go in next week. She said there is a new injectable medication on the market. You take it once a month. But nothing I've tried over the years has worked. It will work for a few weeks, but then it stops. I don't want to get my hopes up."

Sheila nodded. "Totally understandable." She waited a moment to see if Anna would continue.

When she didn't, the therapist changed the topic. "I've been thinking about what you said on your way out last week."

Anna looked at her quizzically.

"You mentioned spending time with Kylie throughout her pregnancy."

Anna nodded but remained silent.

"So since Kylie is gone now, I'm wondering how you feel about the baby? What has that been like for you?" she asked.

Anna started to cry. It was as if the dam holding back her tears suddenly burst. She didn't even realize she still had tears left. As they flowed, the pressure in her forehead intensified, causing her to pinch the bridge of her nose. Sheila gave her space, sitting in silence and pushing the box of tissues across the table toward her.

When the tears stopped, the hiccupping began.

"Oh, I'm sorry," she said between hiccups. "These stupid hic-hic-hiccups." She laughed. "As Kylie would say, 'I'm a hot mess.'"

"You've got nothing to apologize for. I'm sorry if I upset you. What were some of your thoughts or feelings just then? Have you been able to talk with anyone about what's going on?"

"Not really." She shook her head. "Well, I mean a little bit, to Henry." She glanced up at the therapist to see if she was going to interject. Her eyes were kind, and she was leaning forward in her chair, appearing totally invested in Anna's pain.

"It's silly, really." Anna leaned in to whisper.

"What is?"

She sighed, the hiccups now past. "I had this sort of pipe dream."

Sheila raised her eyebrows, waiting for her to continue.

"It's delusional in a way. I guess a part of me was

hoping she would give me, give us, the baby."

Sheila's silence urges her on. "She talked a lot about how much she didn't want to be a mother. She said she never wanted kids but made it clear she didn't believe in abortions. She was going to put the baby up for adoption. I guess I kind of hoped she would somehow consider me and Henry. I was working my way up to asking her. But I felt so stupid, so awkward. What am I supposed to say, 'Hey, Kylie, ya know how you don't want your baby and all? Well, could Henry and I have her?'" She scoffed. "But I never worked up the nerve, and now she's gone."

Chapter 25

Kylie

Kylie was getting out of the shower when the phone rang. After making arrangements to meet the motel manager early the next morning, she grabbed the extra towel and wrapped her long black hair into a turban. Flicking on the TV, she was pleasantly surprised to find an old black-and-white movie playing. She loved old movies. They reminded her of when she would sleep over at her grandma's house. Grandma Rose had a huge collection of classics and was eager to share them with Kylie. One of her favorites was playing, *The Bachelor Mother*. Although Ginger Rogers didn't dance in it, Kylie considered it one of her best roles. She smiled, remembering the times she and her grandmother snuggled under the homemade afghan, eating popcorn. She sat down on the lumpy mattress and was soon engrossed in the story. A soft knocking at her door interrupted Ginger's escapades. Kylie belted her robe and stood on her tiptoes to see out of the peephole. It was the waitress, Aurora.

"I'll be right there." Kylie grabbed her sweatpants and T-shirt and pulled them on. She opened the door.

"Hi."

"Hey, I don't normally bother the patrons," said Aurora, "but since you might end up working here, I thought maybe you wouldn't mind?"

"Do you need something?"

"No." Aurora laughed. "My sister and I are going out for dessert; we thought you might want to join us."

"Oh. Um, that's so nice. Well…" She hesitated. Kylie was unaccustomed to such kindness. "I guess I could join you."

"I mean, you don't have to if you're tired or whatever."

"No, it sounds like fun. I am tired, but some chocolate sounds great right about now." She glanced down at her clothes. "I should change, though. Are you leaving right now?"

"I just got off work, so I'm gonna go home and shower, but I live right around the corner. I can come get you in like forty-five minutes or so."

Why is she being so nice to me? What does she really want?

"Um, sure, okay," Kylie replied with a grin.

****

"This is the best fucking hot fudge sundae I've ever had!" Kylie gushed. The twins laughed as Dawn signaled for the check.

"I still don't know how you managed to eat two appetizers and still have room for dessert! Where do you put it all? You are so thin!" Aurora took the check before Kylie could grab it.

"Nope, it's our treat. We invited you out." Dawn pretended to be stern. Kylie was about to protest but was secretly quite thankful as her cash flow was dwindling. The car ride back to the motel was a quick one. The interior was finally starting to warm up when they pulled back into the parking lot.

"Thank you, guys, so much! I've never met anyone as nice as you. Both of you." She laughed. *Well, one other person was even nicer until, of course, her boyfriend came back.*

"It was fun." Aurora grinned.

Dawn nodded her head and yawned. "See ya around, Kylie. Thanks for coming out with us."

"Thank you for everything. I mean, if it wasn't for you, I don't know where I would be sleeping tonight. Plus, I have a job interview in the morning. I almost forgot!"

"Yeah, we better get you to bed." Aurora grinned at her from the back seat as Dawn jumped out of the car and followed Kylie to the door.

"By the way, Kylie?" She turned to go.

"Yeah?"

"If you end up sticking around, don't break my sister's heart."

"What are you talking about?" Kylie tried to sound naïve.

"I saw the way you were looking at each other all night. I'm not oblivious."

Kylie started to protest, but Dawn interrupted her. "Aurora recently got out of a bad relationship. I don't want her getting hurt again. Don't play with her feelings."

"I understand," Kylie muttered, opening the hotel door. "I'm not planning on hurting anyone."

"They never *plan* on it," Dawn said as she turned back toward her sister.

Chapter 26

Kylie

The next morning Kylie awoke to the soft chimes of her phone alarm. She fumbled in the dark for her cell, squinting against the light of the screen as she turned off the alarm. Grabbing a fresh towel, she stripped and turned on the shower. As she caught a glimpse of her body in the large mirror above the sink, she could see the slight swelling of her belly. She carefully climbed onto the toilet seat to see more of her body. She touched her stomach gingerly at first, then poked it with her index finger. She couldn't deny it; she was showing. Those maternity clothes she packed would come in handy. *I'd better wait until after this interview to let anyone know about me being pregnant. No sense in jinxing things.* As she stepped into the shower, the blast of water stung her breasts. Looking down, she felt as if she was looking at someone else's body. A body more voluptuous than hers. *This is so fucking weird. It's like everything about me is changing all at once.*

****

Cheryl was already at the main desk when Kylie arrived. She was short and stout. Kylie heard the old song "I'm a little teapot" echoing in her head. She smiled, and Cheryl smiled back.

151

"You must be Kylie." Cheryl shook her hand heartily. "The girls are quite taken with you, especially Aurora. I know Dawn could use the help. So, tell me a little bit about yourself. Have you worked in customer service before?"

"Sort of. I mean, I worked in a bar, uh. Serving...customers."

Cheryl hesitated. "And what brings you to Greenville?"

"I guess you could say I'm trying to start over."

"So, you're planning on staying for a while?"

"Well, I don't know for sure, but so far, I like it here. I can't believe how nice everyone is in this town."

Cheryl laughed. "You're not from here, are you?"

Kylie joined in and chuckled. "That obvious, huh?"

"Well, I've noticed New Yorkers always seem to comment about the people around here being super nice. But people who are actually from here don't see anything all that special about the place. I guess I'm glad I'm not a native. It makes me appreciate it all the more. Well, the job is pretty straightforward, it's part-time, but it's also temporary. Our receptionist is taking three months off for maternity leave. Would that work for you?"

"It would be perfect."

"Well, don't take this the wrong way, but I'm used to knowing my employees. It's a small town, and most people grew up together. So, since I don't know you, I'll give you the position on a trial basis. Basically, it means if you mess up, you won't be given any warnings; you'll just be let go."

"Okay."

"I will still be opening and closing the motel, so

right now, I need someone to work the front desk, man the phones, and do the bookkeeping from ten to three. If you think you can handle those responsibilities, the job is yours."

Kylie didn't have to think twice. She had always attracted bad luck, but so far, this little town was becoming her very own talisman. "When can I start?"

Chapter 27

Kylie

It had been three weeks since Kylie stopped in Greenville, and she was already becoming part of a community. The twins wouldn't leave her alone. It was as if she was their pet project. Yesterday, she decided to tell them she was pregnant. Today, Aurora stopped by with homemade cookies, and each of them separately texted her, trying to talk her into allowing them to throw her a baby shower.

"But I'm not going to keep the baby." Kylie was sitting behind the reception desk, going through the junk mail. Dawn was taking her fifteen-minute "non-smoking break."

"Oh wow. Can I ask you why?"

"I can't take care of a baby. She deserves a good mom, who will always love her and always be there for her." She didn't tell her anything about the conception of the child or about her bipolar diagnosis. *Besides, why get too close to anyone here? What if I don't stay?* Prior to meeting Anna, Kylie lived a life of acquaintances, and it suited her just fine. It was easier to keep people at a distance rather than allow them to get too close. Dawn and Aurora were slowly squeezing their way into her heart. They were both so charming and kind. Kylie also had a strong attraction to Aurora, and it was becoming even more apparent the feelings seemed mutual.

"So, what are you gonna do when the baby is born? I mean, you only have, what—four months left?"

"Yeah, I dunno. I guess foster care or maybe adoption?"

"Wow. I give you a lot of credit. It's a bold move." Dawn cracked open her can of soda. On Kylie's first day on the job, Dawn clarified the self-imposed "rules" of her "non-smoking break." She alternated between a soda and a candy bar and a rice cake and water. "That way, I don't get too fat!" She'd laughed.

"A *bold* move?" Kylie could feel her body tense up. She swallowed down a sob threatening to escape. "I see it more as a cop-out."

"No, it shows you are mature enough to put a baby's needs in front of your own."

This conversation was becoming too serious for Kylie. "Or maybe I'm just fucked up." She laughed, broke off a piece of Dawn's candy bar, and popped it in her mouth.

****

After Kylie got off from work, she drove down to the Department of Human Services. She'd been on and off welfare her whole life and wasn't too proud to ask for help. Since she was now pregnant, she knew it was a good time to apply for services. *"Got yourself into some trouble? Not to worry, your food stamps double!"* She winced as she thought of the old saying her mother taught her. *I might as well go sign up for services and find out who I talk to about putting a baby up for adoption.* After waiting in line for over an hour, it was finally her turn.

"How can I help you?" A rotund white woman

with huge breasts and a form-fitting turtleneck stood before her. The shirt revealed lumps and bumps that should not be flaunted. Her nasally, shrill voice made Kylie want to turn around and leave.

"I want to turn in my application for health insurance and WIC. Do you get extra services for being pregnant?"

"Do you have proof of your pregnancy?"

Kylie allowed her fingers to graze against her belly and resisted the urge to make a snide comment. Instead, she pulled out the form from her last OB/GYN appointment.

"Okay. Take these papers to line G." The woman stamped the top form and handed the stack back to Kylie.

"You mean to tell me I waited in line for over an hour, only to be told to get in a new line?" Her voice rose in anger.

"Yep." She sighed. "You have to go through *my* line and get approval *before* you can get in *his* line."

"This is bullshit!" Kylie's voice rose in anger.

A sturdy man in a blue uniform waltzed over. "Ma'am, if you don't lower your voice, I'm going to have to ask you to leave."

Kylie rolled her papers up in her hand and stormed out the door. *Maybe I can come back tomorrow and go straight into line G. How stupid!*

Getting health insurance was vital. She was starting to regret throwing her pills away. Every little thing pissed her off, plus she was starting to feel a bit paranoid. She couldn't get her medication filled in a new town without a prescription from a doctor. Right now, she didn't have either of those things. She was done with work for the day, and the twins were both still working, so she wasn't quite sure what to do with her time. Pulling into the public library parking lot, she glanced around for a spot closest to the door. *No such luck.* Walking was becoming a bit more tiring, and her belly felt like an anchor she had to drag around all day and night. She pulled into a spot between two minivans. Opening her door, she stood and stretched her back. Her eyes locked onto the car seat visible in the back of the adjacent vehicle. A fluffy pink stuffed bunny was beside it. She turned away and slammed her door.

Marching into the old brick building, she stopped inside of glass double doors and looked around for the restroom sign. It was as if her bladder had shrunk to the size of an acorn, and her stomach was a grandfather oak rudely sitting above it.

After relieving herself, Kylie walked up to the checkout counter.

"May I help you?" The librarian peered up at her over her tiny spectacles.

"Um, yeah. So, can I get a library card?"

"Oh, of course, my dear." The old woman smiled. "May I see your driver's license?"

After digging through her purse, which was jammed full of old wrappers and receipts, Kylie was able to find her license. She gave the woman her temporary address, and after clicking away at the computer for what felt like an eternity, the librarian handed her a shiny plastic card.

"You can use your card for books, of course, but we also have a nice selection of movies and music."

"You have movies here?" Kylie glanced around the tiny room. It looked like a library that would have been in Mayberry. "Do you have any old black-and-white ones?"

****

After browsing the shelves of DVDs, Kylie wandered over to the children's section of the library. A blond-headed toddler was standing at the train table. His bright blue eyes looked up at her as she strolled by. He returned his attention to the shiny metal caboose in his hand. A young woman sat on a nearby rocking chair. She pushed a stroller with her foot while scrolling through her phone. A bundled baby peacefully slept while her brother crashed the train cars into each other. Kylie felt indifferent toward them. In all honesty, she felt a bit annoyed at the boy's intermittent noises piercing the room's silence.

Kylie walked over to the shelf marked Parenting. Running her fingers over the spines of the multicolored books, she selected a book entitled *Pregnancy: Loving your new body*. She shoved the book underneath her stack of DVDs and returned to the checkout area. The mother in the rocking chair never even looked her way.

****

As Kylie unlocked her motel room, she balanced her library items in one hand and turned the doorknob. She sighed as she threw the items onto the bed and ran into the bathroom. *Geez! I just peed!* While washing her hands, she heard her name being whispered. She turned off the faucet. The noise stopped. Turning the water back on, she heard it again.

"Kylie. Kylie. Kylie."

She crossed the room, pulling the door open, only to be met by a quiet parking lot. Her car sat alone. Hesitantly, she shut the door.

"Kylie."

What the hell? There it is again. Walking over to the heating unit, she stood in front of it and waited to hear the noise again. Nothing.

Her mind whirled. Her breath quickened. All she could hear was the whirring of the old heating unit. She pushed the panic down into her core and drew a deep breath.

Kylie plopped onto the hard bed, rummaging through the DVDs. She grabbed her favorite Hitchcock movie, *Notorious*, and slid it into the player on a small dresser. Sinking back onto the stack of pillows, she flipped the corner of the bedspread over her legs. Within twenty minutes, she was asleep.

By the time she woke, the room was dark. Black-and-white static covered the TV screen. She grabbed the remote, clicking it off. She shivered in the chill of the air around her. Standing to stretch her back, she startled as someone knocked on the door. She opened the door to Aurora's smiling face.

"Hey. Oh, did I wake you?" Aurora smiled as she noticed a bedspread crease on Kylie's face.

"Nah. I woke up right before you knocked. Come on in."

Aurora breezed through the doorway and tossed her purse on the chair near the bed.

"You know, you really need to find a *real* place to live."

"I know, I know. But the management here is so nice!" Kylie joked.

Aurora giggled. "This lady at my church is renting out her upstairs. Ya want me to get her number for you?"

"Yeah, okay. I mean, sure. Thanks."

Aurora pulled the curtains open and smoothed the bedspread before sitting down. Kylie watched her for a moment before clearing her throat to speak.

"So, how's Dawn?"

"Oh, she's okay. I think it's a head cold. She should be back to work tomorrow."

"That's good. I mean, it's not good she's sick, just that she'll be back soon." Kylie laughed, hoping she sounded less awkward than she felt. "Cheryl said she never calls in sick, so I figured she must be feeling pretty bad."

"Yeah. I'm sure she'll be okay," Aurora answered. She was looking down at her hands while she picked at a rough cuticle.

"Can I ask you something?"

"Okay." Kylie drew out each syllable, taking a big breath. "Did I do something wrong?"

"What? Oh. No. Not at all."

The women sat in silence for a moment, studying each other.

"Well, I guess I wanna clarify something."

"Okay," she said again.

"I know my sister told you I date girls and all…I'm wondering if you've dated girls too?" Aurora stopped picking and grabbed a pillow, placing it in her lap."

"Well, to be honest, I am bi. I mean, I've mostly been with men, but I kinda think they aren't my cup of tea right now."

"Yeah. That's kinda what I thought." Aurora paused and took another big breath. "I'm so not good at this stuff." Her cheeks blushed. "I feel like I'm getting some signals from you, maybe?" Her voice softened.

"How do you feel about me?" she whispered.

Kylie could see her squirming in her discomfort. She liked this feeling of power. Silently, she pulled the pillow away from Aurora. Placing her hands on each shoulder, she eased her onto the bed.

****

Kylie's bladder woke her. She eased her way out from under the sheets and started toward the bathroom. When she returned, Aurora was sitting up in bed. She grabbed her sweater from the floor and was tugging it over her head. She laughed when she saw Kylie watching her from the doorway.

"Are you okay?" Aurora patted the space beside her.

"I'm good. I'm famished but good." Kylie climbed back under the covers and pulled Aurora toward her. "What about you? Are you okay?" She kissed her lips lightly.

"I'm great. Also famished, but great." With a dramatic flourish, she kicked the covers back and scooped her clothes from the floor. "Let's go get some food. I know the perfect place!"

****

They sat across from each other at the small Formica table. Like everything in this town, the diner was old but well-loved. The décor was supposed to be set in the fifties, but the lackluster hot-pink vinyl booths and black-and-white checkered floor left Kylie feeling dissatisfied.

"How old is this place?" Kylie asked as she shoved a heavily salted fry into her mouth.

"I dunno. Pretty old, I guess. I started coming here when I was little. I guess I never thought much about it.

It's been here as long as I can remember. Why?"

"Just curious."

Aurora grabbed a fry off Kylie's plate and smiled. "Can I ask you a question?"

"Uh oh, you know what happened last time you asked me a question…" She giggled.

"I'm serious. I mean, it's a different kinda question."

"Go ahead. My life is an open book," Kylie replied, knowing it wasn't.

"Are you really gonna give up the baby?"

Kylie looked down at her swollen belly. "Yes," she answered, picking up another fry. "You don't think I should?"

"I wouldn't dream of telling you what to do. It's just I know I couldn't do it. Don't take that as a judgment. I don't mean it to come across that way. Having a baby growing inside of me and then giving it away seems way too painful. What about the father? Does he know about the baby?"

"You mean the asshole rapist who took turns with me along with his buddies?" The words tumbled out before she thought to stop them. She covered her face with her hands.

Aurora's eyes widened in surprise. "Oh my God. Kylie, I'm so sorry! I didn't know." She whispered, hoping it would signal Kylie to lower her voice.

Tears began descending Kylie's face. "Well, now you know. And I don't want to talk about it again."

"Okay." Aurora got up from her side of the booth and slid next to Kylie. She wrapped her arms around Kylie until Kylie's shoulders softened, and she buried her face in Aurora's hair.

They sat in silence for a while until Kylie pulled away to wipe her eyes and nose. She mumbled an apology for getting Aurora's shirt wet. Aurora took her hand and held it tightly. Both women sat in silence. When the waitress arrived with the bill, she wordlessly set it on the table. Aurora let go of Kylie's hand to grab the bill.

"I'll be right back." She stood, whisking her purse from the booth.

Chapter 28

Kylie

Sitting on the crackled plastic cushion, Kylie leaned her head back against the smooth wood behind her. She surveyed her surroundings again. Clusters of customers chatted and smiled while shoveling food into their mouths.

What do they all have to be so happy about? Annoyed, Kylie turned to look out the window. A light dusting of snow settled over the cars and pavement. Huge white flakes fell from the gray sky.

"Kylie."

She turned, expecting to see Aurora waiting for her. She was still alone.

"Kylie."

Her stomach tightened as she searched for Aurora's familiar face. Standing, she knocked her ever-growing protrusion into the table as she squeezed out of the booth. As if in a daze, she walked past her friend through the door and out into the wintry wonderland. She stood in the brisk air.

"Kylie."

"Kylie?"

"What?" she turned to see Aurora staring at her. Kylie's bulky coat overflowed from her arms.

"Are you okay? You left your coat. You walked

right past me." She unfolded the coat and placed it over Kylie's shivering shoulders.

"Oh." Kylie laughed. "Sorry, I…I mean, the snow looked so pretty. I followed the call of the wild." She laughed and stuffed her arms into her coat, pulling Aurora close. Their noses now nearly touching. Kylie searched Aurora's cocoa colored eyes. As their lips touched, they locked in warmth, oblivious to the cold around them.

"Come back to my place," Kylie whispered. It was more of a question than a command. Aurora giggled and pulled her toward her car, now covered in a blanket of white fluff. After starting the frigid car, Aurora grabbed her snowbrush and jumped out to clear the fluffiness from the windows. Kylie sat in silence, cupping her hands and blowing warm air onto them. As light crept into the car through the now clear windows, she gasped as she felt a blip of movement inside her. She held her breath and waited. A wispy flutter awoke deep inside her.

"What's wrong?" Aurora pulled the door closed as a white swirl of flakes followed her into the car. She studied the quizzical look on Kylie's face.

"Nothing. I mean, I think I felt some movement."

"Huh?" Aurora's gaze shifted to the hand Kylie rested on her belly.

"Oh. Wow. How does it feel? I mean, how do you feel? Does it make you sad? Angry?"

"I dunno. I mean, I guess it's kinda cool to have something growing inside of me. Maybe I should hate it, but it's not her fault…" Her voice trailed off as she lifted an index finger and traced a heart on the foggy window.

Aurora cleared her throat. "So, do you still wanna go back to your place?"

Kylie pulled her hand away from the window. She eased her hand out of her glove and gently slipped it behind Aurora's neck, pulling their faces close. She answered the inquiry with a soft kiss.

Chapter 29

Kylie

"Good pick! You've got good taste in movies." Aurora scooted her body to the edge of the bed and leaned over to hit the rewind button on the VCR. Once the whirring of the machine started, she crab-walked backward toward the cocoon of blankets they made.

"Very dainty," Kylie joked. "That didn't look awkward at all."

Aurora giggled, smoothing the blankets around her. Kylie's stomach gurgled.

"How are you hungry again? We just ate a few hours ago." She smiled and raised her eyebrows comically. "Seriously, you need to get your own place. You don't even have a mini-fridge here."

"I know. Um, I got some ginger ale outside. Do you want one?"

"What, like in a snowbank? I bet it's frozen!"

"Ha! You're right. What was I thinking?" Kylie laughed as she bent down to retrieve her purse from the floor. She rummaged through the large disorganized bag until she found a half-eaten candy bar.

"Chocolate?" She smiled, breaking off a piece and handing the rest over.

"Absolutely. Got any real food in that Mary Poppins bag of yours?" she asked, shoving the candy into her mouth.

"I've got some boxed preservatives."

"Wanna go to my place? I have an actual kitchen, with a *real* stove and everything!" she joked.

"Mmm, food. You made me an offer I can't refuse." Kylie rubbed an exaggerated circle around the bulge of her belly. "Aren't you grossed out by this?" She tried to pinch the taut skin of her bulging stomach. "I mean, I'm huge!"

Aurora licked the chocolate from her lip and placed her hand where Kylie was pointing.

"One, you're not huge. Two, I think you're beautiful. And three, I hate to break this to you, but you're only gonna get bigger."

Kylie swung her legs over the side of the bed, pushing herself up. *This seems way too good to be true. Something bad is bound to happen soon. It always does.* "You're sweet. I'm gonna shower. Wanna join me?" She smiled seductively.

"You make me an offer I can't refuse." Aurora smiled back as Kylie led her to the tiny bathroom.

****

As they pulled into Aurora's driveway, a light inside the condo flicked on.

"Is Dawn home?" Kylie's voice pitched upward in nervousness.

"Looks like it. Her car is here."

The worn back end of a Chevy peeked out of the darkness in front of them.

"Is she gonna mind me coming over so late?"

"Why would she mind? She adores you. Besides, I got her fries and a milkshake. Come on." Aurora grabbed the large bag of food. Its deliciously greasy aroma filled the car. Kylie followed her up the walkway.

"I guess next time we will have to actually cook a real meal. Burgers and fries are my weakness."

"Next time?" Kylie smiled and raised her eyebrows.

Aurora grinned and unlocked the front door.

Dawn was sprawled out on the couch. The sound from the TV was so loud Aurora had to shout to get her attention.

"Hey, li'l sis, hungry?"

"Ooh, do I smell fries?" She jumped up and snatched the bag.

"Scooch over." Aurora sat beside her twin and shoved her feet under the blanket.

"Hey, Kylie. How's it going?"

"Can't complain," she replied while sitting down.

Dawn stopped mid-fry and stared at both women. She glanced at Aurora, then Kylie, and then back at her sister.

"Oh my God." She straightened up with a big grin on her face.

"What?" Aurora asked with feigned innocence. "What?" she teased.

"Right." Dawn resumed shoving fries between smiles. "Well, it's about time," she said knowingly.

****

The snow continued to fall, and the cozy living room made it nearly impossible to consider going out to face the cold. The three women sat together on the couch. A large, multicolor, knit afghan thrown over their laps. Aurora and Kylie held hands under the blanket as Dawn flipped through the streaming movie selections.

"What do you guys wanna watch now?" she murmured, continuing to scroll past random titles. It was nearing midnight, and Kylie already yawned several times.

"I guess I should get going. I'm pooped, and I have to work in the morning."

"Why don't you stay here tonight?" Dawn pushed the empty fast-food bag onto the floor and stretched her legs out on the coffee table in front of them.

"Yeah, that's totally good with me." Aurora squeezed her hand.

Kylie hesitated. She wasn't used to caring what other people thought of her, but for some reason she couldn't yet identify, she wanted the women to like her.

"Really?"

"Totally. I mean, look at that snow out there. You can crash with me, or if you prefer, you can have the couch."

"Totally. I'll go find you a toothbrush." Dawn stood and stretched. "I'm pretty tired too. I'm gonna head to bed. I'll leave a new toothbrush on the sink in the bathroom for you." She bent to pick up the bag, crumpled it, and walked away.

Kylie pulled her hand away and searched Aurora's face. "Are you sure she doesn't mind? I mean, I don't want to invade your space or anything."

"She's good. I mean, up till now, she's *never* invited anyone to stay. So, I'm gonna guess she likes you." Aurora playfully tasseled Kylie's hair, then smoothed it away from her face. "So, the couch or my bed?" She raised her eyebrows.

"What do you think?" Kylie teased.

Aurora stood, grabbed Kylie's hands in her own, pulled her up, and led her down the hall.

"What about the toothbrush?"

"What? The *toothbrush* is what you're thinking about right now?" She laughed.

Chapter 30

Aurora

Aurora woke with a start. Kylie's arm was flung over her hip. She was murmuring in her sleep. Trying her best not to wake her, she lifted Kylie's hand off her and turned over to view the clock. The digital display read 3:07 a.m. Flipping back around, she snuggled up to Kylie, pulling the blankets closer around them. She drifted back to sleep. The next time she woke, daylight was pouring through her gauzy curtains. Kylie was no longer there. She heard the distinct sound of glass, followed by a thump.

What the heck?

She swung her legs out of bed and hurried to the kitchen. It was empty. Muffled noises were coming from the bathroom. The door was closed. Dawn peeked through her open door. Her hair was ruffled, and she blinked at the harsh hall light.

"What's going on?"

She paused for a moment waiting for an answer, then knocked on the door.

"Kylie?"

The bathtub spigot turned on.

"Are you okay?"

She turned the knob and was surprised to see it wasn't locked. Kylie sat on the side of the tub, facing them. She was still wearing an old T-shirt of Aurora's, but the edge of the shirt was now speckled with blood. Last night Aurora laughed at her when she'd pulled the shirt on. It was so tight it kept scrunching up under her breasts. They joked about it being a maternity tube top. Now the stained shirt was scrunched up over Kylie's belly. Her exposed abdomen was covered with small cuts. The tub was filled with water, and a pile of formerly white towels lay in the bottom of it.

"What the heck are you doing? Are you okay?" The twins rushed over. Kylie was staring down at herself. Blood continued to trickle down the length of her and onto the tiled floor.

"Call 911!" Aurora yelled. She pulled another towel off of the shelf and pressed it against Kylie.

"What happened? Are you okay?"

Kylie looked at her with blank eyes. She pointed at the interior of the tub.

"I tried to wash them."

Aurora reached behind her and turned off the water.

"What? Oh, who cares about the towels! What happened?" She continued to place pressure over the cuts. Dawn ran back into the bathroom, holding her cell phone.

"They're on their way."

Kylie looked up at Dawn and held out her upturned palm. She opened her fingers to display a broken razor blade. Its jagged blue plastic head had been broken off the neck of one of the girl's razors.

The twins glanced at each other for a second before turning their attention back to Kylie.

"Why would you do this to yourself?" Aurora

demanded.

"I'm sorry I ruined your towels." She motioned to the tub again.

"Who cares about the damn towels! Why would you do this? Kylie! Look at me!" She gingerly took the blade from Kylie's hand. The head of it was still surrounded by plastic, but Kylie had still managed to use it.

Kylie reached out toward the blade as Aurora threw it into the corner.

"I had to get them out."

"What? You're not making any sense! Get what out? The baby?"

Kylie looked confused. It was as if she was in a trance.

"The bugs."

"Bugs? What the hell? Kylie, stop! What are you talking about? What bugs?"

Kylie pulled the towel away and tried to stand. By now, a twin was sitting on either side of her. They each held her shoulders, forcing her to stay seated.

"I could feel them moving. They wouldn't stop moving."

Aurora started to cry. She smoothed a stray lock of hair behind Kylie's ear. The three women sat side by side on the edge of the tub, waiting for the ambulance.

****

Kylie's eyes felt too tired to open. Every time she tried, they fluttered shut against her will. It was exhausting to keep trying. She could hear several people talking around her, but it was as if she was too far away for them to notice her. She succumbed to the delicious darkness and returned to her dream.

The next time she awoke, her wrists were bound. She immediately began thrashing. Her throat was dry, and when she tried to call out, the sound was that of a wounded animal. Swallowing, she tried again. She groaned and looked at the soft bands binding each wrist to the side of the bed.

"You're awake!" Aurora entered the room with a cautious smile. Steam was rising from the large white Styrofoam cup in her hand. She set it on the bedside table.

"I'll be right back. I'm gonna go tell the nurse you're up."

"Wait!" Kylie tried to reach for her and swore under her breath. "Why am I strapped to this bed? What happened?"

Aurora leaned over and pressed the call button to get the nurse. Then she sat and scooted her chair closer to the bed.

"You mean you don't remember?"

"What happened? Why am I here?"

"Um, maybe we should wait until the nurse comes in." Aurora reached for Kylie's bound hand and caressed her fingers.

"Fuck waiting for a nurse! *You* tell me! What is going on? Why am I strapped to a bed?" Kylie's voice continued to rise in anger. "Unstrap me! How long have I been here?"

"Since yesterday." Aurora rose as a nurse entered. She stepped away from the bed and stood in silence as the nurse approached Kylie.

"Well, it's good to see you awake. How are you feeling?"

"How the hell do you think I'm feeling? I'm

strapped to a fucking bed! Can't you see I'm pregnant? Untie me!"

"I'm sorry, sweetie, I can't undo them until the doctor changes his orders. Right now, you are being restrained for your own safety." The nurse had an air of sweetness to her voice. Her olive skin and dark hair were a stark contrast against her white uniform. She reminded Kylie of her grandmother in some vague way.

"What do you mean? Aurora, what is going on? What did I do?" Kylie cried. She looked down at the blue blanket covering the mound of flesh. "What did I do?" Sobs erupted from her.

Aurora squeezed her way past the nurse who was trying to take Kylie's blood pressure. After finishing, she stepped away and grabbed the chart from the wall.

"I'm going to page the attending physician." She strode away, the heels of her shoes squeaking against the glossy polished floor.

"The baby is fine." Aurora smoothed Kylie's hair away from her forehead.

"Then why am I here? I don't understand."

"They told me you had some sort of episode? I dunno. You were hurting yourself. You honestly don't remember? We were at my house, and you..." She glanced at the IV pole. "Why didn't you tell me you were...sick?"

"Whatdoyamean sick?" Kylie licked her lips. "I'm so damn thirsty! Am I allowed to drink something here?"

Grabbing the pitcher near the bed, Aurora poured a cup of tepid water into the plastic cup. She lifted it to Kylie's mouth and tipped it gently so she could drink.

"I'm not *sick.* They are sick for tying me down!"

She lowered her voice to a whisper. "Get me out of here!"

"I can't. And you *are* sick. You were cutting yourself. Don't you remember? You bled all over my bathroom." She started to cry. "They found some empty pill bottles in your purse and called your doctor. Your *psychiatrist*." She stretched the word out, and it lingered in the air for a moment.

"Why didn't you tell me you have—issues? They won't tell me much. All I do know is you cut yourself up pretty bad, and they sedated you. The last time you woke up, you started tearing the bandages off, and when one of the nurses tried to stop you, you shoved her!" Tears were streaming down Aurora's face. She grabbed her purse and fumbled around until she found a tissue.

"Luckily, you didn't hurt the baby. The cuts weren't deep. Thank God."

"God?" Kylie spat the word. "Where has He been my whole life? Huh?"

Aurora stood in silence. This was not the Kylie she'd spent the last several weeks getting to know. It wasn't the woman she thought she might even be falling for. Before she could respond, the doctor walked in.

"Hello, Miss Teeter. I see you're awake." His thick black glasses slipped down his nose, and he shoved them back into place while opening her chart. "And you are?" His gaze shifted to Aurora. "Are you a family member?"

"No, I, um. I'm a friend."

"Ah, yes. Well, I have to ask you to leave for a few moments while we have a little chat." He pulled the chair closer to the bed and sat down. Kylie stared at Aurora as she left the room.

"Now then, Miss Teeter. It looks like you are being followed by my colleague for some mental health issues. I see you were diagnosed as having bipolar somewhat recently, and it looks like you were prescribed some medication. Have you been taking your medication daily?"

Kylie gave him an icy stare. "I don't need any medication. Besides, I ran out, and I'm fine."

"I beg to differ." He motioned toward the bed, letting his gaze pause on her arm restraints.

"Right now, you have been admitted to the hospital because you are not only a risk to yourself, but you are a risk to your baby. It looks like you had a manic episode, and until you are more stable and you build up the appropriate medication to a therapeutic level in your system, you are stuck with me." He sat back in the chair and pushed his glasses up again.

"You can't hold me against my will. I have rights," she stated.

"Yes, you do have rights. But some of those rights are—shall we say—*on hold* until you are in a safer frame of mind." He paused and regarded her for a moment. "You will be moving up to the fourth floor, which is our inpatient psych unit. There is a bed available for you later this afternoon."

"How long do I have to stay?"

"Well, it depends on you. If you are compliant with your medication and therapy, we may be able to discharge you to an outpatient program in as soon as one week."

"A week! I can't stay here for a week. What about

my job?"

"Let's take things one day at a time, shall we?"

"Can you take these things off my arms?"

"Can you guarantee me you will not hurt yourself or anyone else here?" he responded.

"Yes," she whispered as he reached for the Velcro strap around her left wrist. The sound of ripping filled her tiny room as he unlatched each band. Kylie pushed her body into a sitting position and pulled at her shirt. "Did I hurt her?"

"According to the ultrasound, everything with your baby looks fine. The cuts were superficial, so there was no risk to your baby." He flipped through her chart, stopping near the back of the plastic binder. "It looks like you are thirty-six weeks along, so just about four weeks until you are full term." He smiled.

"Four weeks?" Her eyes widened in alarm. "Four! I thought I had like two months left! The last imbecile I saw told me I still have a ways to go!" The pitch of her voice was growing uncomfortably high. "What am I going to do?" The rough hospital pillow behind her crackled as she dropped her head back onto it.

"What do you mean?" He snapped the chart closed.

"I'm not keeping it. I have to figure out what to do!"

"I see." He walked toward the door and turned before leaving. "I'll have the nurse page social work. Someone should stop by soon. The social worker will be able to help you. I'll check in on you once you are settled upstairs." Aurora looked up as the doctor entered the hallway. She'd been standing by the nurses' station, scrolling through her phone.

"Will you be visiting for a while?" he asked.

She nodded, solemnly returning to the room.

Chapter 31

Kylie

It turned out the unit they were placing her on was locked. She hadn't even considered being held against her will. Kylie sat on the plastic mattress placed directly on the chilled linoleum floor. Other than a naked pillow, the room was bare. An overhead fluorescent light buzzed and flickered above her. At least she had her clothes back, minus the shoelaces, of course. No potentially harmful items were allowed on the unit. She sighed and walked to the door. It reminded her of the old-fashioned wooden doors she saw in classic Western movies.

I didn't even know they made these *anymore.* She ran her hand over the top of the structure. It was a half-door. The top grazed her stomach, which she observed, must have grown even more overnight. The upper half stood open; a metal hook secured it to the hallway wall. She pushed the lower part open and walked down the bright hallway and into the lounge area.

The space was eerily quiet. A lone woman sat at a small table piecing together a puzzle. She ignored Kylie. The room was large but depressing. Someone attempted to add some cheer to the space by hanging ridiculous-looking curtains bearing tiny rainbows and clouds. A large wooden bookshelf was sparse, populated with a few random books, puzzles, and games. Kylie snickered as she picked up a worn copy of *I'm OK, You're OK.* She'd seen this book countless times at the many used book sales she'd frequented over the years. She shoved it back into place beside a few old psychology textbooks. Kylie had ended up *voluntarily* signing herself into this inpatient treatment, although it didn't feel voluntary. The choices presented were limited ones. She could admit herself to the one-week program and then commit to attending daily outpatient therapy sessions for a month, or they would involuntarily admit her until the doctors determined she was medically fit to make her own decisions. After finding out the baby was due in a few weeks, she wanted to get back to her life as soon as possible. The hospital social worker was scheduled to see her today sometime after lunch.

She left the dreary common room and walked back down the hall to the nurses' station. A large blue paper taped to the wall near the water fountain stated in bold black letters:

Mandatory Group Sessions will be held daily:
9–10 a.m. Self-Harming
10–11 a.m. Art Therapy
11–12 p.m. Eating Disorders
1–2 p.m. Substance Abuse
4–5 p.m. Mood Disorders
7–8 p.m. Trauma
8–9 p.m. Transition

Kylie wondered what they did for people who fell into more than one category. Her therapist had already informed her attending the self-harm, mood disorder, and trauma groups before she could begin her plan to return to the community was mandatory. Visitors were not permitted for the first several days, and she could not leave until she participated in the full week of programming. She was allowed to make two phone calls a day from the nurses' station.

"Can I use the phone?" She interrupted the nurse sitting behind the desk, typing as she sipped from her iced coffee. The nurse peered at her from over her granny glasses and nodded. She continued to type without pausing. Kylie lifted the receiver, but her finger hesitated over the buttons. All of her numbers were programmed into her cell phone. She hadn't memorized any of them.

"Damn it!"

"Is there a problem?" The plump nurse stopped typing and stood up.

"Whadda you care?" Kylie stormed past her and made her way back to her room. She eased her body down onto the plastic mattress. It crinkled under her weight. Sighing, she pulled the stringless hood of her sweatshirt over her head.

****

Aurora stood outside of the double doors and pushed the buzzer.

"Can I help you?" a distant voice crackled.

"I'm here to see Kylie Teeter."

A loud buzz filled the air, followed by a click. Aurora assumed it was her cue to push the door open. Behind the reception desk, a plump nurse sat, playing with her phone.

"Who are you here to see?"

"Kylie Teeter."

The nurse sighed. She stood and walked over to a

rack of blue charts. After pulling one out, she flipped it open and glanced it over.

"She isn't allowed visitors until Friday."

"What?"

The nurse sighed again and returned the chart to the wire rack. "Come back Friday."

"No one told me she couldn't have visitors until Friday."

The nurse sat back down. She pulled her phone out of her scrubs pocket. As she gave her full attention to the little screen, she pointed to a sign posted next to the reception desk.

No visitors are allowed for the first 48 hours of admission.

"Come back Friday."

Aurora paused, then she reached inside her purse, fishing around for a piece of paper.

"Can I leave her a note?"

"Sure." The nurse didn't bother looking up this time.

Her fingers grazed an old receipt. It was wrinkled, but the back was blank. After locating a sticky pen from the depths of her bag, she scribbled a message.

—Dear Kylie, I hope you feel better. Please know I am thinking of you. I'll be back to see you on Friday when you are allowed visitors.

With love, Aurora.—

She folded the note and placed it on the worn countertop. "Will you give this to her, please?"

Looking up, she held her hand out to accept the note and stuffed it in her pocket. "I will."

"Can you at least tell me how she's doing?"

"Nope. Sorry, it's confidential. Come back

Friday." The nurse continued to swipe the small screen in her hand.

Annoyed, Aurora turned and tried to push the handle on the door. It was locked.

Looking up with a sly smile, the nurse punched a series of numbers into a keypad on the wall, and the door clicked. Aurora shoved it open, and with a sigh of exasperation, walked out.

Chapter 32

Kylie

The next two days were a blur for Kylie. Between visits from her new psychiatrist and attending the groups her therapist mandated, she was able to resist the urges to hurt herself. It wasn't as if she had much opportunity. Someone was always checking in on her. Even when she was finally allowed to shower, an aide stood outside the open door. They even refused to let her shave, informing her she could earn the right to use a special razor after her observation period ended. Since she was pregnant, the medications deemed to be safe were limited. Instead, she was not only forced to participate in group therapy, but she had to meet with an individual therapist as well. The focus, they explained, was on cognitive behavioral therapy. Kylie thought they were making it up. Apparently, it was devised to make her change her way of thinking.

One of the hospital social workers came to see her earlier in the day, and she laid out her options regarding adoption. At first, Kylie felt as if the woman wasn't quite convinced she didn't want to keep the baby. But, after she broke down crying and told her about the rape, the social worker didn't question her decision again. She handed her a list of lawyers to help set up a private adoption.

"But I don't have any money for a lawyer." Kylie started crying again.

"It's okay. I'll call legal aid. Let me see if they will take your case. They offer free services if your income meets their requirements."

Kylie brushed her sleeve under her nose. "Would answering phones part time qualify me? It's not like I have a bunch of money hidden somewhere," she scoffed.

"We'll figure something out." The social worker smiled.

****

Today was Kylie's fourth day on the unit. It felt as if she'd been there for weeks, not days. At least today, she had something to look forward to. Aurora was coming after work, and a lawyer was stopping by this afternoon.

Despite all the things Kylie hated about this place, it was surprisingly easy to fall into the routine of life here. Expectations were clear. Wake up at seven a.m. Shower—under the keen observation of an assigned aide, breakfast in the common area, clean up and then attend the litany of groups, individual therapy, journaling, and required meetings. Bedtime was nine p.m., with lights out at ten. Kylie enjoyed the routine, although she missed the comforts of her own space. She was considered a compliant patient and was keenly aware of the rules she needed to follow in order to play their game. Her goal was to be discharged from the program by the end of the week.

****

"Kylie." An aide peeked his head in her room. "You have a visitor." She liked this particular aide better than the rest of them. He was a giant of a man—tall, bald, and covered in tattoos. His shoulders resembled those of a linebacker. His voice was deep, and he spoke in a manner seeming to relax everyone around him. Kylie followed him down the corridor and into the common room. Aurora stood near the bookcase. Kylie paused in the doorway, watching her for a moment. She looked beautiful but terrified. Her hands clasped a small bouquet. While Kylie froze, thinking of what she should say, Aurora noticed her, greeting her with an awkward hug.

"Are you okay?" She pulled back and searched Kylie's face for an answer.

"I'm okay. I'm better than I was."

"I'm glad." Aurora studied the flowers in her hand, then thrust them toward Kylie.

"Here. I thought these might cheer you up. I, I wasn't quite sure what to get you." She reached out to touch Kylie's shoulder but pulled back her hand at the last minute.

Kylie snickered. "You can't catch it, you know."

"What?"

"Depression. Bipolar. Whatever. You can't catch it." She walked over to a folding chair and sat. She locked a foot under a vacant chair beside her and pushed it toward Aurora. It scraped over the waxy floor tiles. "Sit."

"You scared me." Aurora sat down, placing her purse alongside her feet.

They sat in silence for a moment. The wall clock boldly ticked its way into their space.

"I'm sorry. I didn't mean to scare you. Sometimes I scare myself. I stopped my meds. I dunno why. I mean,

I guess I thought I didn't need them anymore. Stupid. It was stupid. I'm sorry." The words tumbled out of her in a rush.

Aurora reached out and took her hand, tracing a small circle into the softness of her palm. "It's okay. I'm relieved you're all right. Listen, Dawn and I talked about it, and we want you to move in with us. I mean, even if it's just for a little while. Until you find your own place, Dawn and I can share a room, and you can take the other one."

Kylie eased her hand away. "So, you don't wanna shack up with a crazy lady anymore?" She raised her eyebrows and then winked.

"I think it would be better if you had your own space for a while." Aurora picked at the edge of her sleeve. Then she looked up at Kylie and held her gaze. "So, do you want to?"

"What? Move in with you guys? Are you kidding? I think you're the crazy ones for wanting me to take over your apartment." She was astonished at the generosity of the offer and couldn't even begin to guess how to communicate her appreciation. "Are you sure?"

"Yes. But we have some ground rules."

"Such as?"

"Wash your own dishes."

"Okay."

"Don't trash our stuff."

"I think I can handle that." Kylie tipped back in her chair. The front legs of it dangled mid-air.

"Lock the door at night."

"Got it."

"Take your medication. And—" She paused dramatically. "—No. More. Cutting." Aurora's gaze fixed on Kylie's.

"Okay," Kylie whispered.

"I'm serious. Don't agree to it if you can't promise. Don't answer me yet. Think it over." Aurora abruptly stood. She bent to retrieve her purse and hooked it over her arm.

"You're leaving already?" The words tumbled out in a bit of a whine.

"I'll be back in a few days. But you can call me. Here, I wrote down my number; I figured you didn't have it memorized." She handed her the ripped-off corner of an old grocery list. "They told me I can come to your discharge-planning meeting. Give me your real answer then." Sternness was a bit foreign to Aurora, but she held her ground. Kylie stared at her as she walked away. Aurora turned back before exiting the room. "I'm making you a generous offer. Don't mess it up."

The baby inside of Kylie gave a sharp kick as Aurora's shoes clicked down the hall.

Chapter 33

Kylie

The meeting with the lawyer was no less stressful. Kylie was relieved to be greeted by a female lawyer when she sat down in the small treatment room beside the nurses' station. The woman introduced herself with a limp handshake, the kind that reminded Kylie of a half-dead sunfish. She tried to let go of her irritation, focusing instead on the woman's words.

"Hello, Kylie. I'm Donna Shareef. Your social worker contacted me earlier this week and explained your situation." Her gaze fell to Kylie's bloated belly. Then she continued, "I understand you'd like to look into setting up an adoption."

"Yep." Kylie smacked her gum. The mint flavor evaporated within minutes of popping it in, but she continued to chew. She could feel her anxiety rising and looked down at her wrist. It was mostly covered by a thin white long sleeve. Above a small tattooed flower, she bore a thick rubber band. She snapped it. The instant sting was satisfying. Her therapist gave her five colored bands and instructed her to use them whenever she felt like self-harming. It didn't offer the same sense of relief, but it did help in some small way.

"So, what do I need to do?" Kylie stood and wandered over to the large black trash can. She started to bend forward, but her stomach wouldn't permit it. Tipping her head over the garbage, she opened her mouth and let the gum fall into it. The lawyer waited for her to finish and return to her seat.

"Well, I guess it all depends on what you want. You can do an open adoption, where you have the ability to contact the family adopting the child. Sometimes, families reach out and send the biological mother photos or drawings. Occasionally, we have situations where the bio mother can actually meet with the child. That would be at the discretion of the adoptive family. Or, you have closed adoptions, where you give up all parental rights, and you have no contact whatsoever with the child or adoptive family." Donna pulled her small briefcase off of the floor and laid it on the table in front of her.

"Do I have to decide what kind of adoption right now?"

"Well, you need to decide soon. It looks to me like you don't have a lot of time left." Donna gave her a small smile. Her tone was serious, but her eyes were kind. "You also need to think about some specifics related to an adoption. Do you already have someone in mind to take the child, or do you want to go through an adoption agency?"

"You mean, I can just give her to who I pick?" Kylie absentmindedly placed her hand on her belly. "Like, if I have someone specific in mind?"

"Well, yes. If that person has expressed an interest and is willing to complete all the paperwork required to pursue guardianship and adoption."

Kylie stared at the large wall clock, each tick seeming to grow louder. *Was everything in my life leading up to this moment in time?* Her breath momentarily caught as she mentally reviewed the events of the last several months.

"Kylie, do you have someone in mind?" Donna cleared her throat.

It was hard for Kylie to tell if she was feeling butterflies or the gentle movement of a baby that didn't belong to her.

Chapter 34

Anna

The letter arrived on an ordinary Tuesday morning. Anna and Henry sat at the kitchen table, each nursing a mug of hot coffee. When she heard the mailman drop her items into the box, she stood and stretched. Setting her cup down, she walked down the hall and opened the front door. Expecting a delivery, she was disappointed to look down and not see a large box sitting on her porch. She sighed and flipped open her mailbox, reaching her hand down and grabbing the stack of mail. As she closed the front door, she flipped through the bills in her hand, pausing at the letter from a law firm.

"I got something from a lawyer." She sat back at the table and flipped the letter over.

"Huh?" Henry was busy reading the paper and didn't bother to look up.

Anna slid her finger into the corner of the envelope and sliced it open. She unfolded the letterhead and tried to make sense of what it meant. Blinking, she licked her lips and re-read the now blurry words before her. The energy in the room changed, and hope descended into the cozy kitchen. Henry looked up in response to the change.

"What's wrong?" Tears were pouring down Anna's face. Henry sat in stunned silence. "What is it?" He stood and walked over. Placing his hand on her shoulder, he peered over her head at the letter in her shaking hand.

"The baby," she whispered. A sob escaped from her, and she covered her mouth.

Henry reached over her and gently started to pull the letter away, but she held it tightly. Letting go, he pulled a chair over to her, motioning for her to sit down.

"I don't understand. What baby? What are you talking about?"

Her hands trembled as she tried to smooth the document on the table in front of her.

Henry bent down to take a closer look. He stared at the paper, scanning the words.

"Kylie wants to give us her baby?"

Anna's throat tightened as she fought the urge to cry again. *It can't be true. It's too good to be true.* She felt like she was outside of her body, looking down at her and Henry.

"Have you even been in contact with her all this time? Is she serious?"

Anna shook her head, then shrugged. She pointed at the letterhead.

"It's from a law firm. Look, it says to call them to set up a time to meet with them."

Henry pulled out another kitchen chair, scraping the linoleum, and for a moment, they sat staring at the letter on the table.

"Why would she do this? I mean, I thought she didn't even like me, much less support us being back together. What if she's not stable? What if she changes her mind later?"

"I don't know. Let's call. We need to find out more information." Anna stood and began looking for her cell phone.

"Wait, let's not jump the gun. I mean, I don't want you to get your hopes up and then to find out she's messing with us or something. I don't want you to get hurt."

Anna paused as her eyes once again filled with tears. "But what if it's true?" she whispered.

Henry got up and squatted down in front of her. They stared into each other's eyes until Anna's grin caused a slow smile to spread across his face. She pulled him close as he rested his head against her stomach.

"Are you sure this is what you want?" he whispered.

"You mean, you don't?"

He looked up at her, shaking his head. "No, that's not what I'm saying—"

"You remember what the doctors said to us after I lost the baby? What if this is our only chance? Our only hope?" He started to pull her toward him again, but she held up her hand in protest. "But, if you're in this"—she lifted her hand, motioning back and forth between their bodies—"for the long haul, then you can't just leave when things get tough," she sighed and stared into his eyes, like before.

"Annie, we've talked about this so many times. You know I would never leave again. I couldn't."

"But how do I know for sure? I never thought you would have walked away like you did."

"I know. I know." He brushed his hand through his hair. "Are we going to have this conversation again?

What will it take for you to believe me?" He grasped her hands. "I'm not going anywhere. I give you my word; I won't walk away. If things aren't right, I promise I'll talk to you before doing anything. We are on the same page, right?"

She nodded, picking up the letter again. Raising her eyes toward his, she gave him a tentative smile.

"Call," he said, pulling his phone out of his back pocket and handing it over.

With a shaking hand, Anna dialed the number on the top of the letterhead. After asking to speak with Miss Rosenbloom, she was placed on hold. She put the speakerphone on, setting the phone back onto the table. She and Henry sat staring at the object while listening to Muzak. Eventually, the phone clicked over to a live voice.

"Hello, this is Jane. May I help you?" Anna nearly dropped the phone, trying to pick it up as fast as she could. Henry motioned for her to keep the speakerphone on. She carefully returned the device to the table.

"Yes, um. Hi. Is this Miss Rosenbloom?"

"Yes, it is. How may I help you?" The voice on the other line sounded friendly but rushed.

"Hi. My name is Anna Johnson. Your firm sent me a letter. It's um, regarding a possible adoption?" Both of their heads were dipped toward the table-bound phone.

"Ah, yes. Thank you for calling me so soon. My secretary sent that letter out yesterday morning. All right, well, I suppose before we proceed any further, I need to ask you a few questions." She paused, waiting for a response.

"Yes?" Anna let the breath ease out of her slowly.

"Miss Johnson, are you interested in pursuing an adoption at this time?"

"Yes. Yes, of course! So, you mean it's real? Kylie really wants me to raise her baby?" Anna's voice rose in excitement.

"Well, there are some specific terms we need to discuss. I wanted to confirm your interest first."

"I am very interested." Anna tried to ensure her voice sounded calm and professional. She didn't want to sound immature or overly eager.

"Wonderful. Well then, the next step would be to set up a meeting with you, myself, and Miss Teeter. Would you be able to meet this Thursday? Miss Teeter is currently at Saint Raphael's Community Hospital in Greenville. Do you know where that is?"

"She's in the hospital again? What happened? Is she all right?"

"She is medically stable. I can't speak to anything else right now. She will be there for a few more days and has expressed interest in meeting there as soon as possible."

Anna looked over at Henry. He nodded and smiled.

"Of course. Yes, Thursday is fine. What time?"

"Let me transfer you back to my secretary. She will set up a time."

"Okay, great. I mean, thank you." The line clicked, and the annoying music returned. As Anna started to speak to Henry, a nasally voice returned to the line.

"It looks like Miss Rosenbloom can meet you this coming Thursday at six forty-five p.m. Will six forty-five work for you?"

"Yes, of course. Thank you."

"And do you know the location of the hospital?"

"I can look it up."

"Wonderful," the woman replied. "She will see you then. Have a good evening." The line went dead.

Anna handed the phone back to Henry, and for a moment, they remained silent. Anna was lost in a world of questions. *Is this real? I don't want to get my hopes up just to be disappointed. What if he leaves again? Can I do this on my own? Does he mean it when he says we are meant to be together?*

Since Kylie's rapid departure, she and Henry discussed the past ad nauseum. Despite her best efforts to appear strong, she always ended up crying in his arms. He'd apologized so many times at this point, she no longer felt the need to dwell on the hurt he had inflicted on her. In retrospect, they'd only had one recent conversation about the future. Any time he brought up the idea of getting married or even engaged, she changed the subject. It wasn't as if she didn't want to marry him. Her hesitation seemed more related to her experience with Kylie. What did it all mean? Was she a lesbian? A bisexual? All she knew was she was beyond confused. When she tried to talk to Henry about her sexuality, he would get more turned on than anything else. He also appeared to be a lot less bothered by the whole thing than she was.

"Why does it matter?" he'd said with a smile. "It doesn't bother me at all if you have the hots for women. I do too!" One time he surprised her by saying if she ever wanted to be with a woman again, he would give her the green light.

"Really?" She tried to suppress her surprise.

"Sure," he said. "As long as I know you're still

gonna stick with me."

Anna cleared her throat, forcing her mind back to the present. "So, what do you think?" she asked.

Henry raised one eyebrow. "It looks like we may get a baby after all." A sunny grin lit up his face.

"It seems too good to be true." Anna felt a familiar sting in her eyes.

"Stop worrying. You know it won't do any good. Besides, knowing you, you're gonna obsess about this for the next two days. Let's meet with them on Thursday and see what happens." Anna nodded in agreement.

"Come on, wanna go see a movie or something? We both have the whole day free."

"I don't think I can concentrate on a movie." She stood, brushing the crumbs from the table into her cupped hand. He followed her to the sink, where she watched them wash down the drain. He stood behind her and wrapped his arms around her shoulders. The embrace felt warm and comforting. Anna gazed out the window overlooking her backyard. Spring was approaching. Tiny green buds poked out of the once-frozen ground. She hadn't noticed the sparrows return, but she watched a few swoop down from the tree and settle on the old clothesline.

"I guess I should start filling the bird feeder again." Her statement broke the silence.

"What? Oh, yeah. I guess so." Gently, he grasped her shoulders and turned her to face him. As she held eye contact with him, she blinked back the tears threatening arrival.

"This can be a new start for us."

"I hope so. I really hope so. But what if—"

He leaned in and brushed his lips against hers, temporarily silencing her doubt.

****

"Come on in," said Sheila as she held the door open for Anna. Stepping in and making her way over to the couch, she felt as if there was more room in here for her to breathe. She inhaled the lavender air and plopped down.

"Thanks for fitting me in on such short notice."

"Of course. What's going on?"

"Well," she began, "I got a letter from Kylie, actually, from her lawyer."

"Oh?" Her therapist pulled her chair a few inches closer to the couch.

"Yeah, so it turns out she wants to meet with us to discuss adoption! I mean, if it's true, it would be amazing!"

"So you don't think it's true?"

"Well…" Anna paused to pick up the wooden coaster from the coffee table in front of her. She regretted forgetting her water bottle in the car. The coaster was smooth; its wood made her think of the old wooden roller coaster she rode on as a kid. Its seats worn smooth from countless kids enjoying the summer sun.

"I don't know what to think. Or how to stop ruminating. It's not like since she hasn't been around I've forgotten about her, ya know. But it's the first time I've even heard from her since she disappeared. She isn't the most 'stable' person, you know?"

"It sounds like you don't trust Kylie. I'm wondering if you also might not trust yourself?"

Anna stopped flipping the coaster back and forth in

her hands and looked up.

"What do you mean I don't trust myself?"

"Well, I'm wondering if part of your hesitation isn't only about Kylie being unpredictable, but of you getting your hopes up and being let down?"

Anna nodded. "Yeah, of course. I'm terrified of even hoping this is real. It seems way too good to be true."

"Mmm-hmm." Sheila sat back in her chair, her eyes shifting from Anna's face to her hands.

The thin layer of bark at the edge of the coaster picked away at one end. Anna followed her gaze.

"Oh my gosh! I'm so sorry. I didn't realize I've been messing with it so much. I can buy you a new one."

"No worries." Sheila chuckled. "You're not the first person to fidget with it…it's fine."

"I'm sorry."

"No worries."

Anna abandoned the coaster on the table and returned her gaze to Sheila's. "What if she is tricking me or something?"

"Didn't you tell me before she was already planning on putting the baby up for adoption? It sounded like she was clear about not wanting to raise it herself?"

Anna nodded.

"Is there any possibility it could be true? Maybe she wants you to be the one to raise her child?"

Anna shrugged her shoulders, trying not to cry. She'd already survived several big losses in her life. She didn't want any more. On the other hand, maybe Sheila had a point. She'd spent so much of her life feeling afraid. Maybe it was okay to hope. Maybe hoping was the point. To fully live, you had to take risks. You needed hope. And you'd get hurt. But maybe, just maybe, all the good stuff made it all worth it.

Chapter 35

Anna

Birdsong woke her the next morning. Their lyrical chatter filled her ears. She stretched and puttered to the bathroom. Henry was often out jogging around the time she woke. She turned the shower on, stepping into it once it reached a blissful warmth. As much as Anna wanted to talk to someone about this upcoming meeting with the lawyer, she didn't. It was as if speaking the words aloud would jinx her. One more day of waiting for her many questions to be answered. *Where has Kylie been all this time? Why is she in the hospital?* And, most importantly, *Does she really want me to raise her baby?* She grabbed the shampoo and lathered up her hair. Rinsing out the suds, she stood, allowing the steady stream to wash over her. Henry's deep voice interrupted her thoughts.

"Hey, can I join you?"

Before she could answer, he pulled the curtain aside and stepped into the shower.

"I'm finishing up." She tried to mask her annoyance. *God, can't I get any privacy?* She loved Henry, but she did not like feeling smothered. Besides, she felt self-conscious enough while wearing clothes. Standing naked under the bright bathroom lights with a razor in her hand didn't exactly make her feel sexy. She relinquished her plan of shaving and gave him a quick grin as she eased her way out of the other end of the shower and grabbed her towel.

"Are you okay?" He peeked his face out at her. She looked over at him and smiled again.

"Yeah, just nerves, I guess."

"Me too." He dropped something, and she heard him swear under his breath. "Listen, I was wondering what you'd think of us heading out there a bit early? I mean, I hear they have lots of little antique shops in the village. Maybe we could even find a used bookstore?" He waited for a response.

"Anna? Are you okay?" He poked his head out again and saw her staring at herself in the steamy mirror.

"What if it doesn't work out?" She turned to him and couldn't help but laugh at the shampoo Mohawk he was sporting.

"What if it does?" He grinned. "Maybe this is our chance? Like, maybe it was all meant to be."

"When did you get all philosophical on me?" Grabbing the hand towel nearby, she wiped the mirror clean. She rubbed lotion on her face, frowning at the faint lines threatening to creep into the space between her eyebrows. Studying her imperfect skin in the mirror, she sighed and grabbed her concealer.

"I mean, *maybe* the whole reason you met Kylie, you *saved* Kylie, was setting us up for this moment in time."

She spent the next few minutes trying to apply her makeup in the precariously foggy mirror. He turned the water off and pulled the curtain open. She tried not to stare at his toned body, and he grinned when he caught her looking. He wrapped a towel around his waist and tried to pull her close.

"Hey! You're gonna get me all wet again!"

"Really?" he teased. She stood still, and he quickly released her.

"I think I need a little space," she said, kneading her fingers into her shoulder. The muscles were tight, and as she squeezed, she became aware of the dull ache in her forehead. "I'm gonna take a walk, and then we can head out. But I like your idea about going early and looking at the shops," she called as she walked away.

****

Despite the car ride being under two hours long, Anna packed a cooler of drinks and snacks. She didn't want something as inconsequential as hunger to ruin her good mood. Besides, sometimes waiting too long to eat was one of the many triggers for her migraines. The walk helped. She tried to focus on what Henry was saying, but after receiving one-word responses to his questions, he replaced his chatter with comfortable silence. It was one of the many things she loved about him. When she needed space, he gave it. He used to be downright clingy. Early on in their relationship, it took him a while to get used to her needs as an introvert. It wasn't until she showed him a comic strip someone posted on social media that he finally could grasp what she'd been telling him all along. The comic depicted a man sitting on a couch. He was alone, reading a book. He looked content and even happy. A large clear bubble encased him. The next portion of the comic showed the same man allowing his friend to enter his bubble. They sat side by side on the couch. They talked. They watched a movie. He looked happy. Then, his friend waved goodbye and left the bubble. The last portion of the comic strip showed the man lying down on the couch, still in his bubble. He looked tired.

"It's how I feel," she explained after he seemed hurt when she turned him down for a chance to go to a bar with their friends. He had gotten mad when she admitted she really felt like staying home and reading.

"You'd rather *read* than be with me?" It was becoming a familiar point of contention.

Even after explaining it wasn't that she didn't want to be with him, she just needed some alone time. He still didn't seem to understand. *Thank God for that silly comic strip!* After she showed it to him and they talked about it a bit, he started cutting her a bit more slack when she asked for space.

She laid her hand on his leg as he drove. They smiled at each other, and Anna turned the radio on. Searching the stations, she settled on classical music. She leaned back in her seat and gazed at the changing scenery.

****

The hospital was easy to find. The village was as tiny as they had imagined. They were happy to kill some time in an antique shop and a used bookstore and even grabbed lunch at a local diner.

"It reminds me of Mayberry," Anna joked, stealing a bit of Henry's apple pie.

"Well—" He licked his lips. "—the sign on the wall says *Best Apple Pie Around for Miles*, and I'm inclined to agree."

"So, you've tasted other apple pies in these here parts?" She laughed.

He raised his eyebrows, dramatically savoring

another bite. "It is kind of a stupid sign. But the pie is good!"

The waitress eyed them warily as they paid the bill. She was cordial but not exactly friendly.

"What's her deal?" Henry muttered as they climbed into the car. Anna shrugged and buckled her seatbelt. She pulled her phone out of her purse and swiped at the screen a few times.

"It looks like the hospital is a few miles from here. We're still gonna be early."

"Not necessarily." Henry backed out of their parking spot. "With hospital parking and everything, we shouldn't be too early. Besides—" He reached over and grasped her hand. "—I can think of a few fun ways we can kill some time."

She laughed. "Do you ever stop?"

"Not really." He smiled.

****

The hospital was much smaller than Anna imagined it would be. The one near their house was an ordeal to navigate. Even though there was a six-story garage attached to their hospital, parking was always a nightmare. This time they followed the signs for parking and pulled into a large lot. A few rows of cars filled most of the spaces nearest to the entrance.

"You sure this is it?" She looked around in astonishment. "It's so small. The lot is half empty!"

"There's the sign. This is the place."

Anna drew in a deep breath, trying to slow her racing heart. They locked eyes, and Henry grabbed her hand.

"It's gonna be okay. Come on, let's go."

She nodded, and they both climbed out of the car.

Chapter 36

Anna

Despite its small structure, the inside of the hospital was impressive. Anna gazed at the beautiful ceilings, graced with paintings of angels, cherubs, and clouds. The walls along the entryway were covered in tapestry, rich with deep burgundy and golden weaving. It was as if an ancient church had been converted into a hospital. As they continued to walk through the main lobby, they passed a small coffee stand. The aroma was sweet and delicious. Anna walked in the direction of the scent, and Henry followed.

"You want another coffee? It'll keep you up," he warned.

"I can get decaf, plus they have donuts!" She peered into the glass case which housed the sugary treats.

"Didn't you just eat?"

"What are you implying?" She frowned.

"No, no. I mean, how can you have room..." He paused when he saw the expression of irritation on her face. "I mean, sure. Sounds good. What can I get you?" He pulled out his wallet.

"That's more like it." She smiled, looping her arm through his. She picked at her sticky bun as they made their way over to the information desk. After Henry clarified where to go to meet with Kylie, they followed the signs to the elevator. Anna paused to roll her pastry bag closed. "Now I can't eat this. I'm too nervous."

"I know what you mean. We'll save it for later. Want me to hold it?"

"No, it's okay." She shoved the bag in her oversized purse. He handed her the steaming cup of coffee. She was grateful to have something to do with her hands as they entered the elevator.

Exiting the elevator, they walked straight ahead to a locked door. An intercom graced the wall next to it. Henry pushed it and stepped back as it buzzed. A crackly voice responded.

"May I help you?"

Henry bent down, placing his face closer to the microphone. "We're here to see Kylie Teeter?"

Anna laughed nervously. Henry turned to look. "What?" he whispered.

"I don't think you have to put your mouth so close."

He shrugged as the intercom buzzed again, followed by a loud click. He grasped the handle and pulled, but nothing happened. They both stood there, staring at the locked door.

"Sir? You need to pull the door open as soon as I unlock it. If you wait too long, it will lock again."

"Oh, okay. Sorry."

The buzzer sounded again, followed by a loud click. Henry pulled, relieved to see it worked. They hesitantly approached the desk.

"Please sign in here." She pointed to a clipboard. Anna picked up the pen and wrote their names under today's date. She noted the lawyer must have already arrived. Her name was written in bold black ink.

"You can take a seat in the common room." She pointed to the left. "I'll go get Kylie."

Anna followed Henry down the hall. She studied the room. Despite the fluorescent lights, it was bleak. A muted TV was secured to the wall. Several chairs were strewn throughout the lonely space. An unfinished puzzle covered the surface of a small round table. Henry pulled a worn chair over to it. Peering around the room, it looked like it was the cleanest option, but Anna was too nervous to sit. She walked over to the bookshelf and tried to appear interested in the selection. Her thoughts raced, and she could feel her shirt clinging to the perspiration pooling under her arms. She opened her purse and grabbed the small tube of lotion she always kept there. Rubbing the jasmine scent into her hands, she inhaled the familiar aroma and hoped it would mask any offensive odor possibly lingering near her. Anna looked up as Kylie shuffled into the room.

"Hey." Kylie smiled at them.

It had only been a few months since she last saw Kylie, but the change was dramatic. Her belly loomed ahead of her, making it difficult not to stare at the protrusion. Her face was clear of makeup, and without the thick black eyeshadow usually coating her eyes, she looked much younger, more vulnerable. Anna could see what she must have looked like as a child.

"How are you?" Anna rushed over, pulling her into an awkward hug.

Kylie smiled and looked down. "Huge."

"No, you look…" Anna paused. "Ready to have a baby soon."

The air between them felt heavy as they stared at

each other in silence.

"Well, I see you're all here." A tall woman, wearing a short dark skirt and a crisp shirt, walked into the room. She placed a thin manila folder on the table and motioned for everyone to sit down.

Kylie cleared her throat and spoke up. "Can I say something here? I mean, before we officially start this meeting?"

"Of course." The lawyer closed the folder and waited for Kylie to continue.

"I don't think we have to be so formal and everything. I'd kinda like to have, like, a real person conversation."

The group remained silent as she continued. "Look, we all know why we are here. I'm gonna have a baby I'm not prepared to take care of, and you *want* a baby. The way I see it, it's a win-win situation."

"It's amazingly generous." Henry's eyes crinkled with kindness as he smiled.

"Kylie, are you positive you want to give up this baby?" Anna dug in her purse for a neglected tissue as her eyes prickled with tears. "I mean, what if you're not *really* sure, or you, I dunno, change your mind?"

"May I?" The lawyer addressed Kylie, who nodded. "Kylie and I have discussed her wishes at length. We would like to propose a private, open adoption."

"What do you mean by *open*?" Anna held her breath for a moment. It felt surreal to be sitting here, in a mental hospital, talking about adopting a baby.

"So here's the plan," the lawyer continued. "Kylie will sign over parental rights to you, Anna. She wants the adoption to be an open one, meaning she will be able to see the child in the future if she so chooses. Of course, we would have to work out the details related to specific fees, guardianship, visitation, and things of that nature."

"It seems too good to be true." Anna reached her hand out, pausing before touching Kylie's arm. "Why me? I mean, why not put the baby up for adoption through an agency or something?"

"Because I know you. And I know you're gonna be a great mom. And you deserve a baby."

"What about Henry?" Anna felt a sudden panic rising in her chest.

"What about him?"

"Well, I guess I'm wondering what will happen if we get married. Would he be able to adopt her too?"

Kylie and her lawyer locked eyes, and Kylie gave a small nod. "Kylie and I have discussed this as well. If the two of you get married, Henry can petition the court to adopt the child as well. However, initially, this adoption will be specific to you, Anna."

"I understand." A slow smile spread across her face. "So, where do I sign?"

Chapter 37

Anna

Anna stood in front of the old vending machine. She wasn't quite hungry, but the throbbing in her head made her think that another rush of sugar might help her feel temporarily better. She'd excused herself from the community room, and after walking down the corridor, stopped in front of the colorful snacks. She'd forgotten about the pastry in her purse and began digging around it to locate a crumpled dollar bill from her purse. She tried to smooth it out before attempting to use it. The hum of the machine was suddenly interrupted by a high-pitched voice.

"Are you gonna get something?"

Anna turned to see a slight girl standing in the doorway. Despite her baggy sweatpants and oversized shirt, she was painfully thin. She had never seen someone so gaunt. She guessed her to be eighteen or nineteen, but it was hard to tell for sure. Her body was that of a child's, but her face belonged to an old woman. Her hair hung straight and limp, grazing the top of her bony shoulders. The skin of her face was taut, and a fine, downy hair covered her cheeks and arms. Anna tried not to stare.

"Oh, um. I'm sorry. Am I in your way?" She stepped back to make room for the woman who looked up at her with a wry grin on her face.

"Not at all. It's not like I want a snack." She motioned down at her skeletal shell. "But I gotta eat something in front of them." She groaned. "Anything to get out of here."

Anna remained silent. She stared at her shoes as if they were the most fascinating things in the world to her. The girl took her time making her selection. Anna wondered if she was mentally calculating fat grams and calories. After she left, Anna walked back over to the front of the machine. She held her breath as she attempted to insert her money into the slot, surprised that the machine didn't spit it back out. She chose a chocolate bar. Chocolate always made things better. Perhaps a bite or two would soothe her anxious soul. When she returned to the room, she could feel Kylie's nervous tension. She gave off a type of kinetic energy. Henry breezed over to her side, and she handed him the candy bar. Now that her hands were empty again, she began fiddling with her ring. The lawyer was gone, and the room had an iciness to it, almost as if the space itself ate away at the pretense of normalcy.

"So, here's the thing," Kylie began. "I'm assuming you guys are together. And it's cool. I mean, if you guys stay together, it's good for a baby to have a mom and a dad, right? Or at least two parents who love each other." Anna and Henry stared for a long moment.

"Yeah. Of course, it would be good," Anna agreed. A hollow scream echoed in the distance. A few nurses rushed down the hallway, past the door.

"It's never a dull moment around here." Kylie tried to make her voice sound light, but that only added to the discomfort in the room. She pulled the edge of her shirt further down her belly as it kept riding up.

"So, what happened? I mean, why are you in here? Are you okay?" Anna whispered these words, hoping the impact of her questioning would soften.

"I kinda went off my rocker again." Kylie moved her finger in an arc near her temple. "I stopped my meds, and it landed me here. But I'm hoping to get out by this weekend."

"Oh. So, do you have a place to stay?" Henry looked at Anna in alarm as she asked this.

"Yeah, actually, I do. I'm gonna stick around here. I've made a few friends. I even got a job. I mean, it's not much, but I like it. It's kinda like a fresh start for me, ya know?"

"I'm sorry to ask so many questions. My mind is racing, and I want to get as much information as I can," Anna continued. "So, how is this supposed to work? I mean, are you just gonna, like, call us when the baby is born?"

"Well, um." Kylie hesitated for a moment. "I was gonna ask if you wanted to be there. For the birth." She squirmed in her chair.

Anna wanted to jump up out of the chair with joy. This was beyond what she ever could have imagined.

"Are you serious?" Her voice wavered with excitement.

"Yeah. But not you." She nodded in Henry's direction. "Only her."

Anna's eyes brimmed with tears. She blinked rapidly, hoping they wouldn't spill over. Kylie leaned forward as much as her stomach would allow. She reached out and grabbed Anna's hands in her own.

"I've messed up a lot of things in my life. But I

don't want this baby to be one of the things I ruin. You've helped me out in so many ways. I mean, you let me, a complete stranger, stay in your house. No one has ever been so kind to me. I've never had this deep desire to be a mom. In fact, I've never even imagined my life with a baby in it. Certainly not *this* baby. You're a *good* person. I know you are. And this baby deserves to have a *good* mom. Maybe even a good dad." She glanced at Henry.

Anna started to speak, but Kylie interrupted her.

"I've spent this whole past week thinking. Thinking about my crappy childhood, about mistakes I've made, about the help I need. And I owe you an apology."

"For what?" Anna whispered.

"For walking away. You didn't deserve that. I dunno. Right now, I'm clear-headed, but I know I'm not always gonna be this way. So, I've gotta make good decisions right now, when the world seems to make more sense to me. I'm so thankful you agreed to take the baby. I'd rather someone I know take care of her."

"Of course!" Tears streamed down Anna's face. She swiped at them as they continued to flow. "Thank you so much! This is just so amazing!" She stood and walked over to Kylie. They looked at each other and laughed before embracing.

Henry excused himself, pretending to be interested in the selection of worn books on the shelf nearby. The women pulled away from each other.

"Thank you so much," Anna whispered.

Kylie nodded and placed her hand on her stomach. "I'm getting kinda tired. I think I'll go lie down for a bit."

"Oh, of course. Do you need anything? I mean, I could run to the store for you. Is there anything you need?"

"No." Kylie chuckled. "I'm okay. I feel like resting. This sounds so weird to say, but my *lawyer* will be in touch with you." She turned and walked toward the door. "And I'll call you when it's time." She started to walk away, then turned once more. "By the way, I found out for sure. It's a girl." Kylie padded down the hallway, leaving Anna and Henry alone in the room.

Henry cleared his throat. "Is she coming back? Is that it?"

"I guess so." Anna smiled with a shrug. "For now. Did you hear what she said? She said it's a *girl*!" She ran over to him as he spread his arms for an embrace.

****

The ride back home was full of chatter. Anna felt a bit euphoric as her words collided with Henry's. Planning for the future was exciting. She asked Henry if they could stop at a baby store on the way home. She couldn't wait to fill the closet of Kylie's old room with tiny clothes. Even the thought of the tiny pink hangers thrilled her. Henry smiled at her enthusiasm, but there was something off about his grin. She suspected part of him felt fearful at the prospect of her getting hurt again.

"Sure, we can stop at the store, but I just feel like I have to get this off my chest."

Anna turned to him in alarm. *I thought you wanted this. Please, don't spoil this for me.*

"I'm so thrilled about all of this. But I'm also scared," he admitted.

"Why?"

"What if it *doesn't* work out? I mean, what if she

changes her mind?"

"Do you think I haven't obsessed over that scenario? I'm terrified too. But the lawyer had me sign a preliminary agreement today. This whole thing, meeting Kylie, *everything* must mean something. Don't you think? I mean, *maybe,* and I'm going out on a limb here, but *maybe* everything does happen for a reason. Ya know?"

"I know. I'd like to think that's true. But part of me is scared it won't work out."

Anna placed her hand on his knee. He glanced over for a moment, then returned his gaze to the road.

"It *has* to work out," she said. "It just *has* to."

Chapter 38

Kylie

She rummaged through her bag for some change. Aurora did her a favor by stopping over at her motel room and packing her some items. She had asked her to grab the jar of coins on her bedside table and was relieved to see she remembered the request. Filling the pockets of her sweatshirt, Kylie felt the loose change jingle as she walked. She flinched unexpectedly when the baby kicked. Instinctively, she placed one hand over the tender spot, rubbing the small knobby protrusion. As she pushed a timid finger into the spot, a tiny appendage of some sort pushed back. She gasped and glanced around as if someone nearby might have guessed what she was feeling. But she was alone in this surreal moment. This tiny life was miraculous. She allowed herself one moment of magic before switching that part of her brain off again.

Stopping in front of the vending machine, she studied her options. Without a doubt, she needed chocolate. She pushed the coins in and hurriedly entered the code. After watching the candy drop down, she grabbed it and ripped into the wrapper. The rich, satisfying taste filled her mouth, and she let out a tiny moan.

The vending machine area was small. It housed one

old but large machine where both sugary drinks and empty calories stood side by side. A black payphone was drilled into the wall. Kylie couldn't remember the last time she saw an actual payphone. She studied it as she continued to stuff the chocolate into her mouth. Someone had etched profanities complete with drawings onto the metal side of it. A lone chair sat beside the barred window. Despite the stained and scratched seat, she plopped onto it. When she'd first arrived, she tried to bypass as much of the disgusting furniture as she could. It was a lost cause. Every area on the unit possessed its own form of filth. Stained chairs, carpets, and sticky tables were the norm around here. It didn't take long for Kylie to stop caring about it. Tomorrow was the day she could finally go home. One more night in this depressing cage, and she was free.

After finishing her candy bar and filling her pockets with more chocolate and chips, she wandered down to the community room. A few new patients arrived throughout the week. A wrinkled old woman sat hunched over a small table. Her wild salt-and-pepper hair reminded Kylie of a skunk. She moved her arms slowly, as if in a trance. Kylie stood and watched her for a moment. The woman was having great difficulty putting the puzzle before her together.

Kylie hesitated before deciding to approach her.

"Want some help?"

The woman looked up in surprise. Her hands shook as she handed a small puzzle piece to Kylie. The two of them worked side by side in silence until a young man approached the table.

Wordlessly, the old woman pushed a small pile of pieces in his direction. The trio continued to work on the puzzle. It was strangely comforting to Kylie. She felt a sense of purpose as she could see the creation forming on the table before them. Every once in a while, she would stretch her back before returning to her task.

"Kylie?" The energy in the room changed.

She looked to the source of the interruption and tried not to appear overly annoyed. She didn't want to do or say anything to jeopardize her release. One of the unit nurses stood in the doorway.

"Yeah?"

"Group is starting. Will you be joining us?" She said it in a way that didn't leave room for refusal. Kylie didn't have to think too much. She planned to do everything she could to ensure nothing stopped her from leaving tomorrow.

"Uh. Yep. I'm coming." She turned from the table and followed the nurse down the hall.

****

"So, for today, we are going to be talking about maintaining wellness." Lynn, the soft-spoken social worker, looked up from her clipboard and scanned the array of chairs pulled into a lopsided circle. She checked the names on her list, noting who was present at today's group therapy.

"To begin, I'd like you each to take a moment of silence and *center* yourself."

Centering was a new concept to Kylie, and she didn't seem to possess the patience to master it. As the group all sat in silence, supposedly clearing minds of negative thoughts, Kylie's hands could not seem to hold still. She began to fiddle with one of the bands around her wrist. Without giving it much thought, she slid two fingers underneath the band and began snapping it against her skin.

The air was filled with the scent of old cigarettes and stale coffee as the group practiced deep breathing. The rubber band now encircled two fingers of each hand as Kylie snapped it back and forth between her hands. The repetition was calming, and soon her worries joined those of the group as they collected above their heads in the charged atmosphere of the room. Suddenly, one of her fingers pulled the band a little too hard, and it flung across the room, landing with a snap against the leg of an empty chair. Eyes blinked open, searching for the interruption. Kylie's body betrayed her as a loud guffaw erupted from her throat. Lynn took an extra deep breath.

"Kylie? What's going on? Do you have something you would like to share with the group?"

Seven pairs of red-rimmed eyes stared. Kylie's laughter grew louder, and a swift kick inside caused her to pause for a moment. Everyone was still watching as she placed her hand on the offending spot and smiled. Kylie tried to hold in her laughter, but another loud guffaw escaped. Kylie laughed again, harder.

The tiny woman beside joined in. Her name tag said *Mary* in a childish scribble. She looked ancient, with wrinkles covering her leathery face. Her white hair bore a bluish tint. She wore enormous blue sweatpants and an orange sweatshirt covered with kittens and mice. She reminded Kylie of the old librarian in grade school. Someone who never fit in, who bore the brunt of adolescent mocking. Mary looked over and smiled. Her face morphed into something beautiful, momentarily illuminating her hidden charm. Kylie paused in her joviality to see if anyone else observed this changeling.

"All right, everyone, let's refocus our energy." Lynn sounded as if she were reading from cue cards.

Back in the present, Kylie smiled and took a *cleansing* breath in, squelching the desire for repartee.

"So, maintaining wellness." Lynn's serious tone caught her attention. "Who can share with the group what you will be doing to make sure you lead a healthier life at home?"

A tiny skeleton of a girl raised her hand. Kylie secretly nicknamed her *Skeleton Corpse* because something about the girl was unnerving. It was a cruel name, so Kylie wisely kept the name to herself.

"Take your meds?" she asked in a voice matching her size, tight and high, with the tiniest whine at the end of each sentence.

"Yes, of course. Many of you are on daily medication to control your symptoms. Taking these medications exactly as they are prescribed is vital. What else?" Lynn looked around the circle, settling her gaze on Kylie. She could feel anxiety creep up her spine, dampening her skin.

"Um, therapy?" Kylie coughed out an answer.

"Yes, Kylie. Thank you for mentioning therapy. Therapy is also crucial for staying healthy. By now, each of you should have been connected up with a primary psychiatrist and a therapist. Can anyone think of anything else that will help keep you out of the hospital?"

The room was silent. Kylie squirmed in her chair, feeling a low ache in her back. Her bladder was already full, but she knew the group ended soon, so she tried to cross her legs. The attempt was misguided as her leg slid back down to the floor. No one warned her pregnancy changes the body in so many large and small ways.

Lynn continued. "I was thinking of something along the lines of self-care. Can someone give some examples of fostering self-care?"

"Eat?" an older woman piped up. Then looking at Skeleton Corpse, she mumbled, "Um, sorry."

Lynn continued. "Making healthy choices is vital. Anyone else?"

"Journal?"

"Yes, journaling is a very healthy way of expressing your emotions."

Lynn prattled on as Kylie watched the clock. Her voice faded as she thought about Anna's visit. Kylie had assumed Henry was coming with her. Even though she hadn't talked to her since moving, Kylie figured Anna and Henry would still be together. This didn't bother her as much as she thought it would. Although, since starting these medications again, she didn't seem to *feel* all that much. It was a comfortable numbness, and Kylie was just along for the ride.

Chapter 39

Kylie

Aurora stood by the nurses' station. She smiled as Kylie walked toward her carrying a plastic hospital bag of dirty clothes. Freedom! No more nurses checking under her tongue to make sure she swallowed the pills. No more disgusting hospital food. The humming of fluorescent lights would be a thing of the past. Most importantly, she could sleep without the interruption of nurses coming into the room to randomly check vitals.

Besides the bright red diagnosis of bipolar, Kylie received a clean bill of health. Of course, she had to agree to weekly therapy and close monitoring of medication. When the social worker met with Aurora and Kylie to discuss the discharge plan, Aurora explained Kylie would be moving in with her and Dawn, and they would make sure the medications were taken daily. Any dignity Kylie possessed disappeared as she nodded in agreement to their plans for her life. She didn't care. She wanted to get out of here. Only a few more weeks and this baby would be born. She would be given a new family, a good family, and Kylie could claim her body again.

"You ready?" Aurora stepped forward and offered to take the bag. She let her.

"You bet I am. Can we order a pizza? I am so

craving pizza. And chocolate almond custard. Mmm." Kylie licked her lips and patted her ever-expanding stomach.

She laughed. "Sure thing, we'll stop along the way."

Kylie smiled as she followed Aurora to the door and waited for the nurse to buzz them back into the real world.

****

"Oh my God, this is the best pizza I've ever tasted!" Kylie reached into the greasy box perched on the back seat. The seatbelt dug into her lap as she stretched her fingers toward the edge of the box. The back of the hatchback was jammed with what could only be politely described as garbage. For being such a meticulous housekeeper, the interior of her car was laughable. Glancing around, Kylie internally shuddered. By no means was she a neat freak, but this was a bit absurd. It wasn't the food wrappers and empty cans strewn about the back of the car disturbing her the most. It was the dark smudges streaking the fabric along the doors. Was it dirt? Trying to be discreet, she adjusted her seatbelt again and looked at the contents of the front seat. Initially, Kylie was so excited to get out of the hospital, she plunked down onto the seat in the car without a second thought. The countless times she had hung out at the twins' apartment, she never thought much about the cleanliness of the place. Compared to the motel room, not to mention a variety of dumpy places Kylie lived in before, their place was a palace.

"You're unusually quiet." Aurora kept her eyes on the road while trying to stretch enough to reach the edge of the pizza box in the middle of the back seat.

"Huh? Oh, what are you doing? I can get you a piece. Hold on."

Kylie handed her a slice and watched a drip of grease drop onto the seat. Grabbing one of the napkins she previously stuffed into a coat pocket, Kylie dabbed at the spot near Aurora's hip.

"Hey there!" She smirked. Her lips were shiny with more grease, and Kylie had a sudden urge to kiss them clean but pushed away the thought and pulled her arm back.

"Are you totally sure Dawn is okay with me staying with you guys?" Kylie asked.

"Of course! If it were up to her, we would have stayed in the same room since we moved in. She wanted to keep sharing and use the spare room as an office."

"Are you sure? Doesn't she want privacy?"

Aurora laughed. Its lightness warmed Kylie's heart. "Not her. We shared a room our whole childhood. She wanted it to stay that way. But I couldn't pass up the chance to have some space to myself." The car shuddered to a stop at the red light.

Kylie looked up in alarm, ready to protest their generosity again.

Aurora held her hand up. "Nope, don't start. We are happy to have you. Trust me. She is more than fine moving back in with me. We set up her old room for you the best we could. My mom let us borrow the old futon from the basement. It's a little bit lumpy, but hopefully, it's okay." She eyed Kylie's belly and slid her gaze over her swollen breasts before pausing at her eyes. Then she cleared her throat and returned her focus to the road. The light turned green.

"Well, thank you again. I mean it. You guys are the best. I really appreciate it. After the baby is born, I can start looking for my own place." The amount they were charging for her share of the rent was less than what she was spending on the motel room, but she didn't want to overstay her welcome.

"We're happy to have you." As she pulled into the complex and parked by the industrial dumpster, Kylie smiled when she looked over at their door. A large *Welcome Home, Kylie* sign was plastered above the entrance. Huge bubble letters were colored in with markers. Whoever made the sign obviously started with big ambitions. The first two words were huge. But the last two letters of her name were squeezed in, with the "e" dangling a bit below the "i."

Resisting a snarky comment, Kylie grinned as Dawn rushed toward her.

"Kylie! Welcome home! Holy cow—you're huge!" She pulled open the back door of the car, grabbing the pizza.

"I mean it in the nicest way." She studied her face as Kylie stuck out her tongue.

"Well, it's true. I am kinda huge. Who knew I could grow so much in a week? It'll be so nice to get my body back."

A silence perched in the air above them as Kylie mutely followed them indoors. The last time she'd been over was when she spent the night with Aurora. Kylie's cheeks burned at the thought of it. Both girls were now shoeless, so she paused and tried to kick her shoes off. They were cheap canvas slip-ons, so now she didn't have to bend over to untie anything.

"I set my old room up for you." Dawn grabbed

Kylie's hands and eagerly pulled her in the direction of the space.

"You guys are the best. I mean it. You didn't have to do this for me." Fighting to keep the emotion out of her voice, she took a deep breath and blew it out. "Thank you."

"No biggie." Dawn resumed her pulling. "Come on. I'll show you what I did."

Aurora grinned and shrugged. Kylie couldn't help but grin back. Despite her best efforts to remain dark and mysterious, she became more of a gleeful fool around Aurora. Usually, pessimism and unhappiness clung to Kylie. Recently, a glimmer of something lighter was taking hold. She was unaccustomed to this feeling. Perhaps it was the drugs.

As Dawn prattled on about how she rearranged the furniture in her room and showed off the new bedspread she found at a church sale, Kylie sat down on the edge of the mattress. A worn copy of *What to Expect When You're Expecting* adorned the bedside table. As she reached for it, Dawn paused in her monologue.

"Oh, I hope you don't mind." She gestured toward the book. "I mean, I know you're not keeping it, but I thought maybe you might, um, want to know what's going on in there." She pointed at the protrusion, then realizing the gesture might appear rude, she closed her fingers into a fist.

Silence filled the small room as they both looked at Kylie. She burst out laughing.

"Going on in there?" She pointed to her stomach. "Well, that's one way to put it." Another laugh erupted, and soon they joined in. As the laughter died away,

Aurora sat down beside Kylie and placed her hand over hers.

"Do you want me to leave?" Dawn made her way toward the door.

"No. I just wanted to tell you again that we're happy to have you here." Aurora motioned for her sister to approach the bed. "You can stay as long as you need to."

Dawn sat down on the other side of Kylie. Looking back and forth between them, Kylie felt tears beginning to well up again. She was *not* a pretty crier, and Aurora knew how much she hated crying.

"Come on; let's let her get a little rest." She stood, and Dawn followed suit. A moment later, they were gone. The comforter was slightly wrinkled on either side from where they'd been sitting. Smoothing it out with her hands, Kylie lay down on the worn cotton. Within minutes, she was asleep.

****

When she awoke, it was dark. Pushing up into a sitting position, Kylie searched the unfamiliar room until she found a small clock on the dresser. Its red numbers were facing away, so she stood and puttered over to it. The clock read 3:47 a.m. *How did I manage to sleep so long?* Kylie's bladder insisted on an urgent trip to the bathroom.

She opened the door and entered the dim hallway. Her feet were silent on the plush carpet. After easing the bathroom door closed, she felt along the wall for the light switch. Once her hands recognized the shape she sought, Kylie flipped on the light. Its brightness temporarily blinded her, and she shut her eyes for a second, then peeked them open slowly. After finishing in the bathroom, she considered returning to her room, but then her stomach growled. Besides, if the pattern of the past few nights were any indication, this baby was awake and on the move, again.

Two nights ago, a sharp jab near her rib cage woke her. It was early morning, sometime between two and three. She tried to go back to sleep, but it seemed as though every position was increasingly uncomfortable. Kylie laid on her back, staring at this lump of an intruder. Suddenly, a jolt of pain shot through as she watched a ripple roll across her stomach. Amazed, she stared at the spot under her T-shirt as the movement repeated itself. The pain was intense, but thankfully it only lasted a few seconds. *I didn't know a baby could…I mean…move so that you could see the actual effect of its motion inside of you.* Despite the constant backache, her bulbous belly, and the inability to go more than an hour without peeing, she was often able to ignore the pregnancy. But, at moments like this, the wonder of it confounded her. It didn't change anything. Try as she might to feel motherly toward this growth, she couldn't. This baby was not hers to keep.

She is not mine. This reminder became her silent mantra.

Chapter 40

Anna

Three days have passed since Kylie's last phone call. Her due date was less than two weeks away. Her former guest room was transformed into a nursery. Over the past few weeks, Henry indulged Anna's desires to paint, decorate, and fill the dresser and closet with tiny clothes. The girls at the salon threw her a soon-to-be-your-baby shower. They chipped in and bought a beautiful car seat and stroller combo. Anna didn't even know such a thing existed prior to visiting the baby specialty store last month.

Looking around the room, she tried to imagine rocking a baby girl to sleep in the plush glider. It was positioned near the window to allow for moon gazing during those late-night feedings. Soon, life was changing forever. And, so far, Henry was along for the ride. *How did I get so lucky all of a sudden? When is the bad thing that's bound to spoil this gonna happen?*

Shaking the darkness away, Anna walked over to the changing table. It was well stocked with newborn diapers and wipes. Everything was in order. There was nothing left to do but wait.

Lately, even on Saturdays, Henry and Anna tried to maintain a tight schedule. For the last few weeks, he had a "honey-do" list hanging on the fridge door.

Somehow the list continued to grow rather than decrease in size. Most of the chores were related to the house. Admittedly, Anna had neglected the place a bit, and despite her feminist leanings, she was secretly thankful he was taking care of those details. Busy work was becoming the preferred way of dealing with any fears about the adoption falling through.

Anna was on her hands and knees in the living room, pushing the child-proof covers into the outlets, when Henry burst through the front door.

"Hey! Where are you?"

"Living room."

His arms were full of shopping bags. "This will solve the problem of the closet." He held one of the bags up in the air.

"Huh?"

"The closet. It's already full of little dresses and stuff. We need to organize it."

"We do?" Anna stood up and stretched her back, eyeing him. "I thought the closet was good." Last weekend, she meticulously hung up a variety of outfits. She even organized them by size.

"No, she's gonna need space in there, for books, and toys, and games."

"Games? You mean like Monopoly? It's gonna be ages before she's old enough to play board games!" Anna laughed.

Henry paused and stuck out his tongue. "I wanna do the closet now. Will you help me carry in the metal racks?"

"Metal racks? Wow. Okay. I was gonna see if you wanted to catch a matinee, but I can see you have something much less relaxing in mind."

"We can do a movie tonight if you want."

Anna followed him outside and stood waiting while he pulled several large white metal racks out of the back seat. He handed her the smallest of the bunch, and they walked back inside.

Chapter 41

Kylie

"What the hell?" Kylie stuck her hand under the blanket and felt the mattress. It was sopping wet. Lifting her hand to her face, she was relieved to see it wasn't covered in blood. She pushed her body into a sitting position. A dark stain covered the gray sheet beneath. Kylie turned to check the neon red numbers on the clock—*3:27 a.m.*

This can't be starting already? I still have half a month to go! Gingerly, she stood and flipped on the light. *I don't even have a bag packed!* Looking around the room, it was apparent she was not prepared for a trip to the hospital. Stretchy maternity pants covered the floor near the bed. The top of the antique dresser was covered with unopened mail. She'd made a neat stack, hoping to figure out a filing system. After weeks of adding to it, the pile toppled over and spilled across the dresser.

Suddenly a sharp pain encircled her body. It felt as if she was being dragged halfway into an elevator, and the door kept closing on her middle. Holding her breath, she squeezed her eyes shut and waited for the pain to subside.

As soon as it did, she exhaled slowly. She was going to need some help. The apartment was eerily quiet. Tiptoeing as much as her huge body would allow, she crept down the carpeted hallway. The twins' bedroom door was ajar. Kylie pushed the door open all the way and walked over to the side of Aurora's bed. She placed her hand on the nearest lump.

"Hey," she whispered.

Aurora jerked awake and sat up so quickly it made Kylie take a step back.

"Huh?" She rubbed her eyes. "Kylie? What's wrong?"

"What's going on?" Dawn mumbled as she reached for the glasses on her bedside table. She fumbled around under the lampshade and eventually turned it on.

"Are you okay?" they both said at the same time.

"I think my water broke."

Kylie watched as their gazes simultaneously traveled down the length of her body, lingering at her crotch.

"But it's too early!" Dawn whined. She jumped out of bed and rushed to Kylie's side. Aurora sat up all the way and threw off the comforter.

"Holy shit!"

"Aurora!" Her sister squinted her eyes admonishingly. "We have to get Kylie to the hospital! If your water broke already, doesn't it mean the baby will come soon?"

"I dunno." Kylie shrugged.

"Didn't you take a baby class or something?"

"Yeah, but I wasn't really paying attention."

Aurora handed Kylie an empty bag and motioned for her to head back down the hall.

"She was too busy flirting with the instructor.

Here, you need a bag of stuff for the hospital. Dawn, will you grab some snacks and start the car?"

"I wasn't flirting." She kicked aside a shoe as she entered her room. "I was appreciating her assets."

Aurora laughed. "You're hopeless." She pulled a drawer open and rummaged through it. "Don't you have more pants than this?"

As Kylie started to point at the pile near the bed, her body recoiled in pain. Grimacing, she eased her way onto the edge of the bed, grabbing a handful of blanket until the band of pain subsided.

"How long have you been having contractions?"

"Not long?" Her voice rose at the last syllable; she was close to tears. She hated herself for being weak in front of Aurora, who dropped the sweatshirt in her hands and was at Kylie's side in an instant. She sat down and started to rub her back. Despite Kylie's resolve to appear stoic, she couldn't hold the tears back.

"It'll be okay. We'll get you to the hospital. Everything will be okay."

Her kindness made Kylie cry even more. An unattractive sob escaped.

"Are you scared?"

Kylie nodded, wiping the tears from her face.

"I'll stay with you," Aurora whispered as she pulled her up. "Let's get you to the car."

Besides Kylie's intermittent groaning, the car ride was quiet. Aurora pulled up to the front of the hospital and parked the car in front of a *No Parking* sign. Before Kylie could protest, she flew out of the car, ran around to the other side, and pulled the door open.

"Uh, I don't think we're supposed to park here." Dawn motioned to the sign.

"Seriously?" Aurora huffed. "Can you run in and grab a wheelchair?"

Dawn ran through the glass doors to the building.

"A wheelchair?" Kylie protested. "I'm not an invalid."

"I know you're not, but don't you think it might be a *bit* hard to walk through the lobby while having contractions?"

The hospital doors swished open as Dawn appeared, pushing a large wheelchair.

"Geez! Look at the size of that thing! I'm not a boat!"

"It was the closest wheelchair I could find." Dawn blushed.

"I think it's one of those bariatric ones." Aurora chuckled. "Hey, can you bring her up to the maternity ward while I go park the car?"

"Of course."

Together, the sisters maneuvered Kylie from the back seat of the car to the oversized wheelchair.

"See ya on the beach!" Kylie motioned toward the beach towel still wrapped around her waist. As they turned to head for the door, another gush of fluid seeped down Kylie's thighs. Aurora was watching from the car. She popped the trunk, jumped out, grabbed an old towel which she threw their way, and was back in the car in a flash.

Rushing through the hospital lobby, Dawn pushed the wheelchair a little faster than necessary. Before Kylie could ask her to slow down, another electric pain tore through her. She cringed and gripped the armrests.

"We're almost there…almost there." Dawn breathed the words quietly as she pushed the button to the elevator. Just looking at her flushed face made Kylie nervous. Small beads of perspiration were forming on Dawn's upper lip. She smiled at Kylie, lips stretched taut as she raised her eyebrows and blew out a puff of air.

"Here we go!" she remarked, jovially shoving the chair inside with a small giggle.

"Calm down." Kylie sighed. "We're not going to the circus."

"Sorry." She giggled again. "I tend to laugh when I'm nervous. You should have seen me at my Aunt Leddy's funeral."

The blast of air conditioning in the elevator made Kylie shiver despite the heat of the day. The unseasonably hot spring weather felt more like a July afternoon. The short walk from the house to the car was oppressive, and daylight wouldn't even be here for a few more hours.

"Are you scared?" Dawn crouched down beside the wheelchair, so her face was aligned with Kylie's.

Before Kylie could answer, the door flew open. A large pink and blue sign welcomed them to the maternity ward. Dawn pushed her over to the desk, where a dowdy middle-aged nurse stood.

"Hi, I'll be right with you."

She bent to retrieve a pack of papers and transferred them to a clear clipboard. Upon closer observation, her skin was flawless, with light brown eyes the color of heavily creamed coffee. Her blue scrubs were not flattering on her pear-shaped figure. Her once dark hair was sprinkled with white and gray and held back with a plastic clip.

"Here you go. I'm going to take you back to triage,

where they can examine you. You can fill out the paperwork there," she said, and Kylie was grateful. Filling out insurance paperwork was always a chore. Doing it while in labor? Nope.

"I'm Charlene," she said, turning around with a slight smile. She looked tired; it must have been near the end of a long shift.

"Hey, Dawn, can I see the papers?"

"Oh, sure." She handed Kylie the clipboard, which she placed on her lap. Kylie pulled the pen out from under the clasp and began jotting something on the bottom corner of the form. Dawn continued to push the chair, following Charlene into a brightly lit room divided by several sets of floral curtains. A few of the curtains were pulled shut, and behind one, a woman moaned. Charlene led them into the closest makeshift room.

"Okay, do you think you can stand and get onto the bed?" She motioned at the twin-sized bed adorned with stiff bleached sheets and a folded blue blanket at the foot of the bed.

"Yeah. I can still walk," Kylie joked.

Charlene smiled. "Okay, then you will need to remove everything and put this gown on. The doctor will come see you in a few minutes."

"My doctor? Dr. Tameca?"

"No. I'm sorry. First, the unit attending will check you to see where your labor progress is, then she will call Dr. Tameca with a report."

"Oh, okay."

Charlene's gaze traveled from Dawn back to Kylie. "Do you need any help getting undressed?"

"No, she doesn't. I can help her." Aurora squeezed

past Dawn and grabbed Kylie's hand. Charlene turned to escape the narrow pod of a room.

"Charlene?" Kylie caught her attention as she walked past the closed curtains to the right of them.

"Yes?"

"Here." Kylie scribbled something on the paper. She ripped the bottom off, folded it in half, and passed it to the nurse.

Tawny eyes held her gaze for a second, and eyebrows raised inquiringly. She took the paper and shoved it into the pocket of her scrubs. Without another word, she was gone.

"Are you kidding, Kylie? Giving out your number while you're in labor?" Aurora didn't even try to hide the jealousy in her tone.

"I wasn't giving her my number, doofus. Just a little note to tell her she is beautiful."

"What?" Aurora and Dawn replied in unison. Dawn laughed uncomfortably.

"It's nothing to worry about. She deserved to know she's beautiful. I don't think she realizes it."

"You're a bit crazy. You know that?" Aurora chided. "Most people get meaner when they're in labor, not nicer. Do you want help getting undressed?"

Dawn watched her sister for a moment, then stepped out of the room, pulling the curtain closed.

"You know this is a super sexy time for me—" Kylie choked on the word as her body froze in pain. Holding her breath, she swatted Aurora's hands away, grabbing at the bedsheet and squeezing it. Aurora was silent until the pain passed. Eventually, Kylie unfurled her hands, staring at the crumpled sheet.

"I can't do this," she whispered. "This isn't even

my baby. I can't do this." Kylie felt her panic rising. "Anna should be here. She should be here."

"Okay. Okay. Let's get you in this stupid bed, then I'll call her."

Chapter 42

Anna

Gasping in pleasure, Anna pulled away from Henry when the phone rang. She tried to force her mind back to him but was unable to stay in the moment as her cell continued to play "Yankee Doodle Dandy." Henry switched her ringtone the other day as a joke, and she kept forgetting to change it. Henry sighed as she sat up and looked at the glowing screen.

"It's Kylie."

"Why are you whispering? There's no one here except for us." He smoothed down the bedsheet and sat up beside her.

"I don't know," she continued to whisper as she stared at the phone in her hand.

"Answer it."

"Hello?" Her voice was strained, so she cleared her throat and spoke again. "Hello?"

"Anna? It's Aurora. Kylie's friend."

"Yes? Is everything okay?"

"Yes. I'm sorry if I woke you, but Kylie wanted me to let you know she's in the hospital."

"You didn't wake me…wait, in the hospital? Why? What happened?" Henry motioned for her to put it on speakerphone, but she waved him off with one hand.

"Well, she's in labor," Aurora answered matter-offactly.

"Labor?" Anna swung her legs to the side of the bed and switched on the bedside lamp. Hurriedly, she bent to collect her clothes from the floor beside her. She threw them into the hamper and motioned for Henry to get up.

"But she still has two weeks to go! How long has she been in labor?"

"I'm not sure; maybe an hour? She wanted me to call you."

"Okay. Let me get dressed, and we'll head out. It takes us about two hours to get there. I'll call you back once we get closer."

"Okay." The silence was thick between them.

"Aurora?"

"Yeah?"

"Thank you for calling me. And thank you for being there with her. She's lucky to have you. See you soon." Anna hung up and turned to Henry.

"You better call into work. It looks like this baby is coming early." Anna grinned as she pulled open her dresser drawer and rummaged around for a decent shirt.

****

The sun was peeking over the horizon as they pulled up to a coffee shop.

"Whaddya want? We're gonna be there a while, right? Might as well stock up." Henry opened the door and grabbed his wallet from the broken cup holder.

"I don't think I can eat. I'm too nervous. But I definitely need some coffee."

He bent to lean back into the car, his eyes meeting hers. Raising his eyebrows, she smiled at his silliness.

"Surprise me," she said with a grin. "But hurry

up!"

"Aye, Aye, Captain!" He winked and saluted her.

Despite her better judgment, she began an internet search on her phone for *preterm labor*. After looking at a few sites explaining what preterm labor looked like, she scrolled down to read about risks. Words like *Autism, Cerebral Palsy,* and *low IQ* danced before her. By the time Henry returned, his arms laden with food, she was crying.

He pulled the door closed, allowing the bag tucked under his arm to fall onto the seat.

"What's wrong?" Concern passed across his face as he eased the coffee into the precarious cup holder.

"What if something is wrong with her?" She sniffed. "Because she's coming before her due date. What if she's disabled or something?"

He picked up her coffee and placed it in her hand.

"Then, we'll love her anyway. We'll love her no matter what. Besides, two weeks early is nothing. No big deal. I googled it." He sounded so confident, she dropped the subject and took a sip of her overheated drink. She cursed silently as the liquid scalded her tongue.

Henry switched on the radio, flipping through stations until he landed on NPR. An old woman stretched out each syllable as she rattled off details of another mass shooting. Anna knew she should pay attention to the newest sensationalized fatality, but the words passed through her without leaving a mark. Her brain buzzed as if stuck on autopilot. It was as if a mantra was stuck on a repetitive loop saying, "Let her be okay, let her be okay."

****

Henry managed to arrive at the hospital in under two hours. It was record time, and Anna was surprised they weren't pulled over for speeding.

"Do you want me to drop you off at the front?" Henry paused as he pulled into the main parking lot.

"No, I want you to walk in with me. I'll call Aurora and let her know we're finding a spot."

Breathless with anticipation, Anna dialed the number she still knew by heart, reminding herself it would not be Kylie who answered. While Henry squeezed into a spot meant for a compact car, she wrote down the details of Kylie's whereabouts. She was admitted, and according to Aurora, she was already five centimeters dilated.

"What does that mean?" Henry asked as he opened Anna's door for her.

"Well, the least descriptive answer would be her body is getting ready to deliver a baby."

"Okay. Well, let's go then." He grabbed her hand, and they walked toward the hospital.

Chapter 43

Kylie

"Get the fuck away from me!" Kylie yelled. Aurora pulled her hand away from Kylie's damp back. Her eyes prickled at the harshness of the words.

"Where's the nurse? She said I could have an epidural!"

Aurora took a step back as if it would protect her from Kylie's wrath. "She went to get the special doctor, the one who does the epidurals."

"Well, what the hell are they waiting for? For me to rip in two?" Kylie demanded. Before Aurora could respond, the nurse entered the room. Her presence exuded serenity. The sweet smell of lavender followed in as she stood beside Kylie.

"How ya doing, Kylie? Can I get you some ice chips? I know you're in pain, sweetie. The doctor is on his way. He'll be here any minute to give you the epidural." She plumped the pillows behind Kylie's back and helped her ease back onto them. "I'm gonna need to check you to see how far dilated you are now. Okay, sweetie?" Kylie nodded grimly as the nurse grabbed gloves from a box on the wall. "Would you like your friend to step out?"

Aurora headed toward the door.

"It's nothing she hasn't seen before." Kylie

snorted.

"Kylie!" Aurora's pale cheeks flushed.

The nurse paused, looking back and forth between the two women. She smiled as if she possessed a secret knowledge. "Ah. All right then. Just lie back. You might feel a bit of pressure here." Kylie reached for Aurora's hand as the nurse lifted the edge of her gown.

Other than the sound of the baby's heartbeat displayed on the monitor beside the bed, the room was silent.

"All right, sweetie. You're making nice progress. I'd say you're a good seven centimeters dilated."

"Is that good?" Aurora asked.

"Well, it means she's moved from early labor to active labor. We're a step closer to meeting your baby." The nurse smiled sweetly. White and gray wisps of hair curled around her face. The remnants of her younger self were slipping out of a messy ponytail.

Aurora squeezed Kylie's hand. Kylie already felt exhausted, and the main brunt of the labor work hadn't even started.

"It's not my baby."

The nurse opened her mouth to speak but then remained silent.

"Can I still get an epidural?" Kylie asked.

"That's up to the doctor to determine. Oh, hello. Can I help you?"

Anna stood in the doorway. Her face was drained of color. She wore wrinkled jeans and an oversized T-shirt.

"Hi, I'm...I mean, the nurse up front said it was okay to come back. My name is on the list." Anna's voice rose, showcasing her anxiety.

They looked at Kylie for some sort of signal.

"Yeah, this is the baby's mom."

Anna's face lit up as she moved to Kylie's side.

"Kylie? Do you want me to leave?" Aurora looked uncomfortable.

"Of course not! I need you here with me!" She squeezed her hand.

"Hello. Hello all. I'm Dr. Sankar. Wow, you've got quite a crowd in here!" The doctor pushed a small silver cart into the room with him.

"Kylie, I'm gonna need at least one of these lovely ladies to step out while I give you your epidural."

"I'll go." Anna and Aurora replied simultaneously.

Kylie gripped the side rails of the bed and groaned. She squeezed her eyes shut as the doctor nodded for both women to leave the room. Anna and Aurora stood on opposite sides of the hallway. Even with the door closed, they could hear Kylie swearing. Aurora smiled.

"She's pulling out all of her best words for the occasion."

Anna laughed. "Yep, that's Kylie for you."

Each woman silently regarded the other. Aurora resisted the temptation to pull out her phone and busy herself.

"How long were you two together?" she asked Anna.

"Oh, um, not long. I mean, I'm not sure we were ever really *together*."

"Oh, but she said…well, I guess it doesn't matter now." Aurora hoped this didn't sound rude. She hadn't meant it to sound harsh. "Um, I only meant—"

Anna interrupted her. "No, it's okay. I get it. Listen, I wanted to tell you…" She paused and lowered her voice. "She *needs* to keep taking her meds. Can you help her with her meds? I can't stress enough how important this is."

"Yeah. We talked about it. A few weeks ago, when she was having a good day, she wrote down what she was taking for me. She has an appointment with her psychiatrist next month."

"Okay. Thanks. She's lucky to have you in her life. I mean, I'm happy for you guys."

Aurora blushed. She hated having her emotions show so easily on her face. "She's lucky to have you too, ya know. I mean, with the baby and all. It's good it's gonna be an open adoption."

Anna nodded as Dr. Sankar pulled the door open.

"Come on in, ladies. Kylie said she wants both of you here for the delivery. She's getting closer. So, I've asked the nurse to call me in about an hour or two. In the meantime, she should be feeling much better. Try to keep her happy. I'll be back."

Kylie lay on a stack of fluffy pillows. She smiled as they approached the bed.

"Holy shit! This is some good stuff. I mean, this is like *the best* invention ever!"

Anna laughed. "Well…great! It sure works fast!"

Aurora smoothed out the blanket and sat on the side of the bed. "My mom said whatever medicine they gave her before the epidural made her all goofy. Apparently, she started seeing dog heads on everybody in the room!"

The room erupted into laughter for a few seconds, followed by silence.

Aurora began rubbing Kylie's foot as Kylie closed her eyes in pleasure. Anna looked uncomfortable and turned to retrieve a chair. As she pulled the chair closer to the bed, she cleared her throat.

"Are you sure you want me here?"

"What? You don't wanna be here?" Kylie chided. "Don't look so worried. Of course, I want you here. I want you to hold her right away." She paused as if searching for words. "So she can recognize her mother."

"Kylie, are you sure this is still what you want? I mean, you can always change your mind," Aurora said. Anna held her breath. Aurora picked up her other foot and began kneading Kylie's arch.

"Of course, it's what I want. I'm not ready to raise a baby. Anna is. And, if I want to see her in the future, I can."

"Of course you can! That's why it's an open adoption." Anna rushed to reply. "You can be as involved as you want to be."

Suddenly the monitor started beeping. The nurse rushed into the room, followed by several wide-eyed residents.

"What's wrong? What's going on?" Strangers soon surrounded Kylie as Anna and Aurora were forced to step back.

"Kylie, the baby's heartbeat is dropping. We want to make sure she's not in distress. I'm going to page the doctor, but in the meantime, I need to see how much you've progressed."

"Can you send all these people away?" Aurora could see the panic in Kylie's gaze.

"These are students, we are a teaching hospital, so they are here for their residency to learn—"

Kylie cut her off. "As much as I *love* an audience, I

don't really want my v-jay-jay to go viral!"

Before Kylie could continue, the nurse motioned for the students to go into the hallway. As soon as they did, Aurora returned to her side, grabbing her hand. Kylie held out her other hand to Anna, who hesitated for a second, then took it.

The women looked down at the floor as the nurse reached for Kylie. With a few swift movements, she felt around. Pulling her hands away, she peeled off the gloves and threw them into the red bin near the wall. Anna looked up too quickly, noticing blood on the fingertips.

She broke the silence. "Is everything okay?"

"I'm sure it will be fine. Kylie, it looks like you might be ready to start pushing soon. Since the baby's heartbeat is a bit low, we want to get her out soon. We don't want her to be in distress."

"Pushing? Already?" Kylie's brazen demeanor disappeared. "I thought you said it would be like another hour?" She looked like a scared little girl. "How do I push if I can't even feel anything down there?"

"Well, it's kind of like pushing as if you were having a bowel movement. Your body will know what to do."

"What if the baby *is* in distress?" Anna whispered.

"I'm going to connect this small wire to the baby's head, so we can better monitor things."

"You're sticking a wire up there?" Kylie tried to scoot her body back up to a semi-sitting position. She quickly gave up.

The nurse smiled. "It's a small wire we will tape to the top of the baby's head. I'm going to go call the doctor, and then I will be right back with everything." She quietly left the room.

Aurora and Anna each stood by the side of the bed.

"It's gonna be okay." Anna's voice filled the space between them.

"Of course it will be okay. And we'll stay with you the whole time," Aurora said.

The nurse rolled a metal cart back into the room. The top of the tray contained an assortment of items they didn't recognize.

"All right, Kylie, Dr. Tameca is on his way. In the meantime, why don't we see how your little girl is doing, okay?"

"She's not mine." Kylie glared at the nurse. Then she softened her tone. "She's Anna's."

"Of course. I'm sorry. Do you want Anna and…" she paused as if searching her memory for a name.

"Aurora." She stood as she spoke her name aloud.

"Yes, Aurora. Do you want them to stay?"

"Yes."

Chapter 44

Kylie

The next several minutes were silent, except for the beeping of the heart monitor. The screen also showed a bar graph indicating when a contraction began and stopped. They all watched the monitor as a contraction appeared to peak.

"You seriously don't feel that?" Anna was incredulous.

"Nope. Like I said: Best meds ever."

They all chuckled.

Dr. Tameca entered the room. He bore a sense of friendly confidence, yet his manner was calm and kind. "Well, all righty, Miss Kylie, it looks as though we might be ready to have you start pushing."

He walked to the foot of her bed, pulling a thin strip of glossy paper from the bottom of the monitor. Studying the graph, he clicked his tongue. Then, realizing he was doing it, he stopped and looked Kylie in the eye. "It's time for this baby's birthday. So, here's what we're going to do. I'm going to put the side rails of this bed up, and you can grip them for extra support if you want. Then, when I tell you to—push. When I say *stop,* you need to stop until I tell you to start pushing again. Okay? Does that sound like a plan?"

Kylie nodded. "So, you want me to pretend I'm

taking a dump?"

The doctor laughed. "Yes, well, that's one way of looking at it." One by one, he pulled the side rails up until they clicked into place. Then, the nurse eased a long metal pole out of the rail near her. She swiftly swung it above Kylie's chest and hooked it onto the other side of the bed rail. It reminded Kylie of a vacuum cleaner extension.

Dr. Tameca grabbed a stool on wheels and placed it at the foot of the bed. As he sat down, the nurse placed her hand on Kylie's exposed knee.

"Kylie? If it's all right with you, I'm going to support your leg, and one of your friends can hold the other one while you push. All right?"

Kylie nodded and looked at Aurora, who responded by placing both hands on Kylie's knee and giving it a light squeeze. Anna looked around uncomfortably as if she wasn't sure where to go.

"Dr. Tameca?" Kylie motioned toward Anna. "This is the mother. She can watch the baby come out. Give her to Anna when she comes."

A slow smile crept over Anna's face as the doctor motioned for her to stand beside him.

****

"Push, Kylie! Come on, push!" The nurse turned into a coach, and her co-captains were cheering her on. She was trying to follow their instructions to push for what felt like ages. Her legs continued to tremble, even when she was resting between contractions.

"Kylie? You've been pushing for almost an hour. The baby's head is ready to crown. If she doesn't want to come out in the next few pushes, I think we will have to talk about a C-section. Neither of you can keep this up much longer."

"A C-section?" She panted. "No. I don't want a C-section!" Her voice was shrill with emotion.

"It looks like another contraction is coming up." He studied the monitor for a moment. "When I say push, push with all your might, but make sure you stop when I tell you. All right?"

As instructed, Kylie pushed as much as she could. Her legs continued to shake as she grabbed the bar above her, now slick with sweat.

"I see her head!" Anna gasped, resisting the urge to jump up and down with excitement.

"You're doing great, Kylie!" The nurse looked up at her face before peering under the sheet again. Her head is nearly through! Do you want to reach down and feel it?"

Kylie shook her head and frowned.

"All right, one more big push, and she should be here. Wait…wait…okay, push!"

Kylie thrust every ounce of energy she had left into it. She pushed and pushed and pushed, not hearing the voices around her. The room was a blur of random colors and noises as if she woke up on a merry-go-round. She hated merry-go-rounds. It wasn't until the nurse touched her face she finally heard the words, "Stop! Stop pushing!" A quick look passed between doctor and nurse as she let go of Kylie's leg and moved next to Dr. Tameca. Kylie fell back onto the pillows. Tears slipped down her cheeks.

"Is she out?" she whispered.

"Yes. It's a healthy baby girl. We need to cut the umbilical cord. Do you want to do it, Kylie?"

"No." She turned her face away. "Let Anna."

Anna stepped forward as the nurse placed gloves on her outstretched fingers. She looked at Kylie but turned back to the doctor when Kylie ignored her. He mimed what to do with the scissors and handed them back. Slicing through the rubbery substance, Anna detached the baby from Kylie. Dr. Tameca held the baby out.

"Do you want to see her?" he whispered to Kylie.

Kylie sobbed as she turned her head away. "No. Give her to Anna."

Chapter 45

Anna

Dr. Tameca handed the baby to the nurse, who motioned for Anna to follow her to the other side of the room. After weighing, poking, and prodding, the baby was deemed to be healthy. Kylie hadn't named her yet, and Anna wasn't quite sure what the protocol was. She and Henry hadn't talked much about names. They assumed Kylie would name her.

When the nurse finally handed the baby over, Anna thought her heart would burst with love. The tiny scrunched up red face was the most beautiful creation she had ever seen. Anna wanted to kiss her perfect bow lips and never let her go. She gently stroked the impossibly small fingers and studied her miniature form.

After cleaning up the area, the nurse motioned for Anna to place the baby in the mobile crib and follow her out of the quiet room. Kylie lay in silence with her face turned away from them. Anna closed the door as they walked down to the nursery. She and the nurse each held a side of the mobile crib as they squeaked down the hall. The wobbly wheel didn't seem to bother the baby, who was sleeping sweetly. Anna paused in her journey, which caused the nurse to stop her steady pace and glance up.

"I, um…can I go get my boyfriend now? He's in the waiting room."

"Yes, of course. We will be"—she pointed to the nursery—"right there."

"Okay, I'll be right back." Her fingers grazed the top of the crib as she walked away.

She hadn't found Henry in the waiting room. Rather, he was tucked away in a tiny lounge crowded with three huge vending machines. Somehow, he managed to doze off while sitting in a hard plastic chair wedged between two machines. Anna guessed the low hum encompassing the room lured him to sleep. Approaching quietly, she nudged his shoe with hers. He jolted awake.

"Hey. How is she?" He stood and cleared his throat.

"The baby is here. Do you want to meet her?"

"Of course I do!" He gathered his belongings, laying in a crumpled heap underneath the chair. As he transferred all of his items to one arm, he grabbed her hand. She led him back through the waiting room, pressing the button for allowance into the unit.

"What's her name? How's Kylie?"

"Kylie didn't name her yet, and she didn't want to see her. She wanted us to leave the room." Before he could press her for more details, she knocked on the thick glass windows. Nearly a dozen portable cribs stood in a row. Only four of them contained bundled babies.

"Which one is she?"

"Right there. The one on the end. See where the card above her says, *Baby Girl*?"

His face lit up, the smile staying on his face while

the nurse opened the door.

"You must be *Dad*." The nurse gave him a small wave. Henry continued to beam. "We haven't had a situation like this in a while, so we do things a little bit differently with adopted newborns. I'm going to bring the baby out to you. In the meantime, you can make yourself comfortable in this room." She motioned toward a tiny room adjacent to the nurses' station. As she opened the door again, she paused. "I'm Charlene, by the way." Henry pumped her arm up and down as he shook her hand vigorously. She laughed. "I'll be right back."

Charlene led the way while Anna pushed the crib, and Henry walked beside her. The room was small, with barely enough room for the expandable loveseat. Instead of a chair or dresser, a tall and thin plant stand stood in the corner. Waxy green leaves sprouted out of a decorative white pot. For a split second, Anna wondered who remembered to water them. Upon further inspection, she realized they were fake.

"Babies often stay with us for a few nights while mom is recovering. So, I'm sorry the room isn't better. I'll leave you to settle, and I'll be back in a bit. But, if you need anything, come out to the nurses' station." She turned to go.

"Are we sleeping here?"

"Honestly, I've never been here for a newborn adoption before. We put a call into the supervisor, but I suspect she'll want us to monitor the baby for at least one night. So, you are welcome to stay, not that there is much space to sleep. The loveseat does fold out into a small bed if you need it."

"Can we see Kylie?" Anna bent over the crib and

touched the tip of the baby's knit cap. The hospital staff had placed a cozy pink hat on her head.

"She won't let anyone in the room right now except for the medical staff."

"Is she okay?" Henry asked.

"I'm sure she'll be fine. So, let us know if you need anything. I'll be back with an update soon."

"Thank you," they replied in unison.

Chapter 46

Henry

Even with a brand-new baby, there are only so many hours one can study her. After tucking her crib up next to the bed, Anna lay down beside her. Henry tried to stretch out also, but since part of his body was hanging over the edge of the bed, he managed to plaster himself to Anna's side while one leg dangled below. His foot firmly planted on the floor braced the weight of his body and kept him from falling. They lay there for a few minutes, aware of the dull beeping and voices murmuring from outside of the room. Soon, Anna nodded off. A faint smile was still pressed to her lips, the tips of her fingers grazing the side of the crib. Henry eased his way off the bed and tiptoed to the door. Flipping the light switch off, he pulled the door closed as he stood in the hallway.

He found the twins in the waiting room. They were leaning against each other, shoulders touching. Although they both looked exhausted, Aurora had taken the brunt of the excitement. She sat up as Henry approached.

"Hi." Her voice was weary, yet alert.

"Hi." He sat down next to them, which prompted her to sink back into the padded high back.

"How's Kylie?"

"Not good," Dawn replied. "I mean, medically, she's okay. Tired, of course, but…"

"She kicked me out." Aurora's voice rose. It sounded like the beginning of a whine. Her sister grabbed her hand, and they both inhaled together, paused, and exhaled in unison. He wondered if this was some sort of twin calming technique they used.

"The lawyer is on her way. She's going to go over the paperwork with her in a few hours. I guess the nurse said she'll call us."

"You guys should go home and get some sleep."

Dawn looked at her sister knowingly, as if they had discussed this already, and she was waiting for Aurora to give in and agree to go home. Neither of them asked about the baby.

"When I called the lawyer, she said she'll come find you guys after she meets with Kylie." Dawn stood, pulling her sister up. "We're going to go home and rest. Call Aurora's phone if you need anything, okay?" Her voice was weary from hours of sitting in a waiting room full of strangers. Henry knew the feeling.

"Okay. Thanks." He watched them exit, thankful he had thought to exchange numbers earlier in the day. He wandered back into the tiny room. Anna was sitting up in bed, a white bundle in her arms.

"She woke up." She grinned. "I changed my first diaper." She nodded to the tiny bulge placed on the edge of the bed.

"Sorry I missed it." He surprised himself by realizing he was sincere. He lifted the wrapped-up diaper and tossed it into the trash by the door. He sat beside her, and she handed him the baby.

Epilogue

Kylie

Why does everyone keep asking me if I'm okay? All these people keep coming back and asking if I'm sure about my decision to give her away. Why wouldn't I be sure? Do you seriously think I want to see her face every day and be reminded of how she got here? She didn't ask to come into the world this way, and she deserves a better life than I can give her. Stop fucking asking me! I signed the paper. Now leave me alone! Maybe someday I'll want to see her. Aurora keeps telling me that I can always make plans to see her in the future. Maybe she's right. But for now, I simply want to start over again.

Aurora is still here. Even with all my pushing away and swearing and mood swings, she still stays. She stays when no one else ever has. She cares about me for some reason. Here she is now, bringing me a fistful of pills everyone says I have to take. I'll take them, for now. I admit it does help me step back and breathe when I get so angry I want to tear at my skin and find my stashed kit to carefully cut the hidden parts of me to soothe and ease the pain.

No one's found my small kit yet. But it's there, in case I need it. For now, I just want to sleep. I'm so tired. But Aurora? She's still here.

Sara Zavacki-Moore

****

Anna

"Let's go back to something you said a few minutes ago," Sheila urged. "Remember when you said something to the effect of how you felt heavy? Can you tell me more about heavy?" Anna sighed, leaning back further in her chair. She glanced at the clock, noting the few minutes left in her therapy session.

"Well, it's kinda like when you were a kid at the dentist, and you wore a big lead apron to get an X-ray done. Ya know? I feel like I'm wearing that apron around all the time."

Sheila leaned forward. "Is there anything that makes the apron lighter?"

Anna paused and whispered, "Charity."

****

Life is surprising. A year ago, I would have never predicted I would save a stranger. Yeah, things got messy. Life is confusing. It's full of random happenings that somehow change our fate. When Henry left, just when I needed him the most, my heart hardened. Sometimes it's easier to keep people at a distance, to not let them see the mess I am inside. All of my quirks, my crazy thoughts, and my pain haven't scared Henry away, though. He's still here. When I think I've finally figured things out, the universe laughs and scrambles everything up. Now, look at this beautiful baby. We've been given a second chance. Kylie's been given a second chance too. I hope she decides to remain in our lives somehow. She didn't even want to name the baby. But I knew as soon as I saw her scrunched-up little face. Charity Grace will grow up knowing love comes in all forms. Sometimes it comes when you think the world is dark, cold, and mean. She'll learn that showing kindness and generosity can change the course of a life forever. She'll learn so much. And I can't wait to start teaching her.

A word from the author...

My love of reading and writing started at a young age. Both offered me a multitude of opportunities for creativity and escapism.

Despite being an introvert, I adore performing on stage. Community theater, singing, playing my ukulele, or improvising are outlets from the stressors of everyday life. I spent many years working as a social worker, and I now have a small private practice as a hypnotherapist. My husband, children, cats, and bunny live with me in upstate New York.

Visit with me at:

www.facebook.com/ZavackiMooreChoosingCharity
https://sarazavackimoore.wordpress.com/
www.hypnohelpservices.com

Thank you for purchasing
this publication of The Wild Rose Press, Inc.

For questions or more information
contact us at
info@thewildrosepress.com.

The Wild Rose Press, Inc.
www.thewildrosepress.com

www.ingramcontent.com/pod-product-compliance
Lightning Source LLC
Chambersburg PA
CBHW051538260626
47170CB00003B/997